The Day Of The Rascal

A HUGO DARE ADVENTURE

DAVID CODD

PROLOGUE

I usually find sitting still quite boring.

Walking. Running. Hopping. Skipping. Yes, they're all well and good. I'm even partial to a spot of shuffling sideways like a crab. Or taking really long strides that run the risk of splitting my underpants.

Sitting still, however, is a different beast altogether. I don't like it. And, as far as I can tell, it's not overly fond of me either.

Until today …

I hadn't shifted an inch since I had first removed the blindfold. That was partly because my bum had gone numb, but it was also because I was too afraid to move. Moving, as far as I could tell, could easily result in the unfortunate death of either my good self or my equally good friend and Chief of SICK, the Big Cheese.

Why? I hear you ask.

Oh, you didn't. Never mind. I'll tell you anyway.

Somebody was pointing a gun at us.

The room was dark and my eyes hadn't quite adjusted properly, but I was fairly certain that the shadowy somebody

I could just about make out in the opposite corner was a man. He was wearing a long coat and a trilby hat that covered much of his face. And a gun. Don't forget about the gun. He wasn't wearing that, though. He was just holding it in his hand. Armed and dangerous and ready to fire.

'Help me ... please ... I don't deserve this ... I'm far too important for such nonsense!' With a blindfold still covering his eyes, the Big Cheese threw his hands in the air and hit me where it hurts. 'Is that you, young Dare?' he cried out.

Yes, that was me. Young Dare. First name Hugo. Codename Pink Weasel. Agent Minus Thirty-Five. SICK's youngest – and finest – super spy. Thirteen years old, but who's counting? Not me, that's for sure. Although I can. Count, I mean. I know all the numbers. At least forty-nine if I put my mind to it.

Right, that's enough about me. Don't look like that. You know far too much already and the book has barely begun.

'I'm right beside you, sir,' I whispered. 'I've not moved a muscle.'

'I think you'll find that's not strictly true,' argued the Big Cheese. 'What about your lips? And your tongue? As for the rest of your puny body, maybe it's time I found out for myself ...'

The Big Cheese finally mustered the courage to pull the blindfold from his face. He seemed to regret it the moment he spotted the gun.

'Oh, cripes,' he muttered under his breath. 'That's unfortunate.'

'Unfortunately so,' I nodded in agreement.

'At least we now know what will happen if we try and make a run for it.' The Big Cheese made a *popping* sound like a bursting bubble. If that was his best attempt at a gunshot then I was bitterly disappointed. A *crack*, yes. Even a *snap*. But definitely not a *pop*. 'Let's just wait here and see what happens,' the Big Cheese suggested. 'He might get bored and wander off. Or just fall asleep. Either way, I'm easy.'

I kept my head still, but let my eyes drift around the room. 'I've been here before, sir,' I remarked, 'and I don't think we've got anything to be afraid of.'

'No, not much,' groaned the Big Cheese. 'Only the man with the pointed gun. Still, there's only one way to find out for sure if he's the dreaded Rascal we've been searching for …' The Big Cheese took a huge breath. 'Are you the dreaded Rascal we've been searching for?' he bellowed at the top of his voice.

'Why don't you speak up a little, sir?' I moaned. 'I'm sure there's one person on the other side of Crooked Elbow who didn't quite hear you the first time.'

'Zip it, young Dare,' growled the Big Cheese. 'I think the Rascal is about to answer.'

He didn't.

Not only that, but he didn't move. Not in the slightest. Not even a flicker or a flinch. A shuffle or a sway. A blink of the belly button or a tap of the toenails. In fact, as far as I could tell, he wasn't even breathing.

'He's a dummy,' I blurted out.

'Bit rude,' mumbled the Big Cheese. 'We don't want to upset him.'

'You can't upset something that can't hear you,' I explained. 'And that dummy can't hear me because he hasn't got any ears. Or eyes. Or a nose. He's not real. He's straight out of a shop window. Let me prove it—'

'Permission denied!' cried the Big Cheese, as I clambered to my feet. 'I know exactly what you're going to do … and I'm ordering you not to!'

'Oh, don't be like that,' I said. 'We're not going to get shot. No way. Not on your nelly. I'm one-hundred-and-eighteen-per-cent certain of it. Sometimes you've just got to trust me.'

'Young Dare …' warned the Big Cheese.

I was halfway across the room when the Chief of SICK jumped up and tried to grab my arm. At the same time there was a loud *crack.* Now, that was more like a gunshot. Nothing like that strange popping sound.

I turned in horror as the Big Cheese slumped to the ground, clutching his chest.

Whoops.

That wasn't supposed to happen.

The Big Cheese had been shot … and it was all my fault!

1.'WHY ARE YOU HIDING FROM ME?'

I want to take you back to a time before blindfolds and gunshots.

Don't worry; we're not going far. Just fourteen hours and seventeen minutes to be precise. Nothing to get your tonsils in a twist about. Listen, I wouldn't do it if I didn't have to ... but I do ... so you might as well get used to it.

What's that? You have? Good. I knew you wouldn't want to make things any more awkward than they already are.

Allow me to set the scene. It was four forty-one in the morning and I had just been rudely awoken by the hideous howl of two cats ripping the hairballs out of each other. They were in the garden; right outside my shedroom. That's a shed-cum-bedroom for those of you who aren't familiar with the concept. It was where I lived. Through choice, I might add, even if I do have to share the limited floor space with a filthy assortment of plant pots, compost, and the occasional uninvited snail. For obvious reasons, I was still drawn to the family home from time to time, mainly to eat and wash and visit the lavatory (although I rarely just visit these days without leaving some kind of unwanted gift). Still, when all is said and done, my shedroom is the perfect place for a highly-skilled super spy like me to get my head down and stay out of trouble when I'm not undercover. And if it wasn't for those pesky cats, that was exactly what I would have been doing now.

Sitting up in bed, I vigorously rubbed my nostrils until I remembered it was my eyes that I was supposed to be rubbing and my nose just needed a good pick. Once I had done both to an adequate standard, I climbed feet-first into my dressing gown and hung my slippers from my ears. Yes, it was early and, yes, I was still half-asleep, but the day hadn't got off to the best of starts.

Not to worry. I had a cure for that. It began with *break* and ended in *fast* and I knew just where to find it.

The cats had stopped arguing, shaken paws and become the best of feline friends by the time I had squeezed past the lawnmower and stepped out into the darkness. It was a revoltingly cold morning, but I wasn't planning on hanging around outside long enough to feel the chill penetrate my pyjamas. Instead, I bounded across the garden as quickly as possible and headed towards the house.

Also known as thirteen Everyday Avenue.

Let me take a moment to introduce my parents, Dirk and Doreen Dare. One was the tea boy for secret organisation, SICK (not to mention the greatest spy who never was) and the other was my mother. Maybe that's a little harsh. Admittedly, she, too, had her own unique set of skills. One was moaning, whilst the other three were fussing, nagging and complaining. Unfortunately, she was an expert in all and only showed signs of improving with age.

With food on the brain (and, no, I don't mean I was balancing a pumpkin on my forehead), I made it to the house in record-breaking time. My hunger, however, had distracted me.

Senses down, I made the first of three mistakes that a spy like me should not be making.

Mistake number one – I didn't realise that the back door was slightly ajar.

With my eyes glued to the grass for any sign of fresh bottom deposits from those pesky cats, I carelessly pushed the door to one side and walked straight into the kitchen without thinking twice. Or even at all. Oh, it's like that, is it? Let's get one thing straight. It's not my fault my mind always takes a few moments to start up in the morning. Or even a *lot* of moments. It has been known to not wake up at all if I'm being honest. It just hibernates for a few days; recharging its batteries for when it's really needed.

Mistake number two – I failed to notice that there was a light on in the kitchen.

Barely able to muster the strength to lift my own eyelids, I closed the door behind me, wiped my slippers on the mat and then set to work searching for breakfast. From left to right I began to raid the cupboards for any sign of my favourite cereal.

Drum roll please …

Multi-grain, choco-frosted, crunchy-crispy, sweet and

sour, loopy hoops. With added prunes. And a hint of garlic.

They're a bit of a mouthful in more ways than one, but utterly scrumptious once you've got used to the taste. Persistence is the key. It took me three long years, but I've never looked back since.

The cupboards were practically overflowing, but that didn't mean they were practically overflowing with the cereal I craved so badly. I switched to the drawers, but the result was the same. Then I moved to the fridge. Then the sink. And finally the oven. As a last resort, I checked inside the washing machine, but it was no use. The packet wasn't there. The cereal had vanished.

'Why are you hiding from me?' I muttered under my breath. 'I'll find you eventually. I always do.'

Not true. I searched in all the same places again, but still didn't stumble upon anything that even half resembled it. So, that was that. Game over. I had tried … and I had failed. Beaten by a breakfast cereal. How embarrassing!

Throwing my hands up in despair, I plonked myself down at the table without looking, all the while pretending that I wasn't that hungry anyway. Curiously, it wasn't a chair that I landed on, but a human.

A real life, fully-formed, large and lumpy man to be precise.

That was my third mistake.

There was somebody else in the kitchen … and I had just tried to sit on them!

2.'THAT'S STRICTLY NEED TO KNOW.'

I jumped up in fright before stumbling on the spot like a ballerina on a banana skin.

Then I fell over.

Poor form, Hugo. Very poor form.

It was only when I had clambered back to my feet that I finally got to take a look at the man who was in my kitchen. Sat hunched over the table, his head was down and his elbows were up as he shovelled huge spoonfuls of breakfast cereal into the ginormous hole in the centre of his face. That's his mouth, in case you're wondering. Not any other ginormous hole that he happened to possess—

Whoa! Did I just say cereal?

Yes, I did. To my dismay, the man was munching on multi-grain, choco-frosted, crunchy-crispy, sweet and sour, loopy hoops. With added prunes. And a hint of garlic.

My favourite.

How dare he?

I studied him a little closer and it became perfectly

apparent why he dared. The man was big. Bigger than big. About three-and-a-half times the size of me, he had meaty muscles, fat fists and a gargantuan gut that strained against the buttons of his shirt. His hair was white in colour, his beard was thick and his nose was redder than a reindeer's in a tanning salon. Appearances can be deceptive, though. This cereal-stealing lump was no Santa Claus. He wasn't even the Easter Bunny.

But he *was* trouble.

I could smell it a mile off. That and rotten cabbage. Although, I have to confess, that particular stench was coming from yours truly. Just nerves, I guess. You can hardly blame me.

Yes, this bulging-bellied blob was an uninvited intruder, and, yes, I should really have asked him to leave, but for some reason I chose not to. Maybe it was fear. Fear of being rolled up like a pancake and then swallowed in one huge gulp.

I made a snap decision to scarper before I went the same way as my favourite cereal. I had barely lifted my slippers, however, before any chance I had of escaping was extinguished altogether.

The Bulging Blob wasn't alone.

Lurking behind the kitchen door, like an exact opposite of his larger than life companion, was another man. Toothpick thin like a … um … toothpick, his hair was disappearing fast from his head, his skin was marked with scratches and scars, and his eyes were practically non-existent. Given the choice, it was the kind of face you'd happily lock away in a cupboard. Not ugly as such. Just untrustworthy. In an ugly kind of way.

I smiled. Why not? It's easier than frowning and, besides, I didn't want them to see how nervous I was. 'Can I be of assistance, gentlemen?' I asked politely.

Toothpick looked over at the Bulging Blob, who, in turn, glanced up from his bowl. 'No,' he grunted.

'Okay.' I couldn't help but shuffle awkwardly on the spot. 'It's just … you know … this is my house … and I was thinking … oh, I suppose it doesn't matter … except … I have no idea who you are … or why you're in my kitchen … eating my cereal … my *favourite* cereal. So, have you got names?'

'Names?' The Bulging Blob stopped munching for a moment. 'Yes, we've got names.'

'And so have I,' agreed Toothpick, unnecessarily.

'That's a start.' The kitchen fell silent. I waited for exactly twenty-two seconds before I spoke again. 'Oh, you want me to guess? Well, let me see. This shouldn't be too difficult. How about … *Tom? Or Dick? Or Harry?* Or even Dom or Nick or Larry? Or maybe—'

'Brown Cow,' said the Bulging Blob, interrupting me. He gestured towards the door with his spoon. 'And that's Grey Hound.'

'And I'm Grey Hound,' repeated Toothpick. Maybe he was hard of hearing, but he always seemed to be at least a second or seven behind every conversation. Either that or he was just incredibly stupid. Which, the more I looked at him, probably seemed the most likely answer.

'Lovely names,' I grinned. 'A colour followed by an

animal. It reminds me of something, but I can't quite put my finger on it. I'm Hugo, by the way. Hugo Dare.'

'We know,' said Brown Cow.

'And so do I,' added Grey Hound.

Interesting. I had no idea why these two goons were in my house, but the fact they both knew my name suggested they were here for one reason and one reason only.

Me.

'Don't take this the wrong way, Mr Cow and Mr Hound,' I began, 'but the time has come for me to bid you a fond farewell. It's nothing personal … or maybe it is … just a tiny bit personal. Anyway, I've got things to do … lots of things … I just can't quite remember what they are right now—'

'I don't think you understand the situation.' It must've been serious because Brown Cow put down his spoon. 'We're not going to stop you from leaving so you don't have to make excuses.'

'You're not?' I said, confused.

'We're not,' repeated Brown Cow.

'And neither am I,' added Grey Hound.

'In fact, we want you to leave,' continued Brown Cow.

'And so do I,' added Grey Hound.

I screwed up my face. 'You do?'

'Of course we do,' nodded Brown Cow. 'We want you to leave … with us!'

'And me,' added Grey Hound.

Brown Cow looked over at his partner. 'Just let me do the talking, yeah?'

It took a few seconds before Grey Hound eventually replied.

'I think I'll just let you do the talking, yeah?' he suggested.

So, I was right. Brown Cow and Grey Hound *were* here for me.

And now it was time to find out why.

'Before I go anywhere, I think it's only fair that we get to know each other a little better.' I sat down at the kitchen table, although on this occasion I chose a different chair to Brown Cow. 'Don't panic; the questions won't be too challenging,' I said. 'Nothing to make your brain explode. I was just wondering … what is it that you actually want with me?'

Brown Cow poured another generous helping of cereal into his bowl. 'That's strictly need to know,' he muttered. 'And *you* don't need to know.'

'Oh, it's like that, is it?' I sighed. 'How are we ever going to become the best of buddies if you won't tell me anything? Would you like me to give you a second chance? Who sent you?'

'That's strictly need to know again,' said Brown Cow, plunging his spoon into the bowl, sending milk spurting over the sides. 'And *you* don't need to know … again.'

'This is ridiculous,' I snapped. 'You're not going to tell me anything, are you?'

'I can tell you why we're here.' Brown Cow held my stare as he continued to munch away on my favourite cereal. It was making me feel hungry, although not hungry enough to pick at the bits that were escaping out the corners of his mouth. 'We're here to collect you,' he explained. 'Collect and deliver.'

'Collect and deliver?' I shook my head. 'I'm not a parcel. Why would anybody want me delivering?'

'You're special.' Brown Cow raised a thick eyebrow as he looked me up and down. 'Believe it or not, but you're a special delivery,' he said unconvincingly.

The funny thing was, I did believe it. Now, I'm not one to blast on my own trombone, but I *am* special. All the way from the scabby soles of my feet to my messy mop of hair. I was the super spy with spots. SICK's secret weapon. Although I do sometimes wonder if anybody outside of my shedroom actually realises this.

'Is that it?' I shrugged. 'Is that all you're going to tell me? I suppose everything else is—'

'Strictly need to know,' finished Brown Cow.

'Of course it is,' I groaned. I didn't have to put up with this kind of nonsense. Not in my own kitchen.

So I decided not to.

'Let this be a warning to you,' I said sternly. 'When the clock strikes five, I'm going to make my move. It will be both swift and brutal. Inevitably, the two of you will get hurt. *Badly* hurt. Like *crying for your mummy* hurt. Big tears and lots of snot. Do you understand?'

Brown Cow burst out laughing. Several seconds later and Grey Hound did the same. Unfortunately for them, they seemed to find me funny. That was their mistake. They wouldn't be laughing soon.

'You're going to make a move at five o'clock?' A grinning Brown Cow scanned the walls for any sign of the clock I had mentioned. 'What time is it now?'

I had no idea, but I wasn't about to tell him that. If I'm being honest, there is no clock in the kitchen. Not anymore. Not since my father had taken it down the last time the room had been redecorated.

No, the clock was just a ruse. The faintest of feints. A simple deception to leave both Brown Cow and Grey Hound looking in the wrong direction.

Now I was ready and they weren't.

Ready to make my move.

Advantage, Hugo Dare.

3.'GET IN!'

What I'm about to tell you is top secret information.

Highly sensitive. For your eyes only. So, if you're reading this out loud then stop. I said *STOP*. You have stopped, haven't you? Good. Then I'll proceed.

I've got skills.

Lots of skills.

Skills seeping out of my armpits. Dripping off my tongue. Trickling out of my nostrils.

I can punch, kick, jab and block. I can twist, turn, swerve and swivel. I can slide, glide and ride the tide. I can spin around on my head without getting dizzy. Okay, maybe a little dizzy, but not enough for me to pass out. I can even bend over backwards and stick my feet behind my earlobes whilst reciting the alphabet.

In the end, I decided not to try any of these skills when I finally made my *move*.

First, I leapt up onto the table, grabbed the cereal packet and threw the remaining contents straight into Brown Cow's face. As expected, he dropped the spoon and lifted his hands up to his eyes as my favourite loopy hoops seemed to momentarily blind him. What I didn't expect, however, was for him to topple backwards off his chair and hit the wall with an almighty *thud*. That was an added bonus.

One down, one to go.

The kitchen was still shaking as I turned sharply, flicked out my slipper and deliberately knocked the milk carton straight onto the floor. Grey Hound charged forward, oblivious to the puddle that had formed by his feet. He slipped and then slipped some more until, inevitably, he slipped over.

The whole move had taken less than five seconds.

Less than five seconds for me to put both Brown Cow and Grey Hound on their bums.

Two down, none to go.

I hopped off the table, side-stepped the milk and then left the kitchen as quickly as I could. My plan was to exit the house via the front door. Simple.

Or so I thought.

I had almost made it across the hallway when I heard a voice coming from the top of the stairs.

'Really, dear, do you have to make such a horrendous racket at this time of the morning?'

It was my mother.

'Don't blame me,' I pleaded, 'blame … blame …' Skidding to a halt, I glanced back into the kitchen. Brown Cow and Grey Hound were beginning to stir. Soon they would be back on their feet. 'Oh, just blame me,' I said hastily. 'You usually do anyway. Now, if that's all, Doreen, I think I'll be on my—'

'Wait!' ordered my mother. 'Please don't call me Doreen. We're not friends; you're just my son. Is that clear, dear? Well, is it? You are listening, aren't you?'

Of course I wasn't. If I'm being honest, I had already pulled opened the door and dived outside before she had even started talking. In hindsight, I don't know why I bothered to dive. I probably could've just walked out like a normal person. At least that way I wouldn't have had to waste time peeling myself and my pyjamas up off the driveway. I could even have closed the door behind me. And locked it.

As it was, I was still scrambling to my feet when I heard the grunts and groans of two advancing goons.

Brown Cow and Grey Hound had left the kitchen.

And the house.

And now they were right behind me.

Run, Hugo, run.

I strayed off the driveway and zig-zagged across the front garden instead. The hedge was high, but I took a breath and vaulted over it with ease. My feet stumbled as I landed on the pavement, but not enough to stop me from checking both ways before I rushed into the road. Sure enough, there was a squeal of screeching brakes followed by a furious flash of light as a car pulled up noisily beside me. A rear door opened without warning.

'Get in!'

The voice was coming from the driver's seat, but it was too dark inside to see who was doing the talking.

I sensed trouble behind me. Unsurprisingly, Brown Cow

and Grey Hound had chosen the driveway rather than the garden hedge. Now they were on the pavement. Almost within touching distance.

'Get in!' repeated the voice in the car.

It was an option and, at that very moment, probably the only one I had. Crouching down, I threw myself onto the rear seat and slammed the door shut. 'I'm in!' I shouted. 'Now let's go!'

I sat up and waited. The engine was still running, but the car refused to move.

'I said go!' I yelled. 'Go, go … no!'

The door swung open and Brown Cow shuffled in beside me. I was halfway out the other door when he gripped hold of my pyjamas and pulled me back towards him.

'Just relax, Dare.' Cereal fell from his mouth as he spoke. 'This is our car,' he revealed. 'And that's our driver. Thanks for doing as you were told. You've made things very easy for us.'

'And me,' said Grey Hound, climbing into the passenger seat.

I was about to protest when my eyes were suddenly switched off and I was plunged into darkness. Brown Cow must have put something over my head. Stiff like cardboard, it felt greasy against my face. I was about to remove it when my wrists were squeezed together.

'This won't take long,' Brown Cow insisted. The car jerked to life and I fell back against my seat. 'Just sit still and be quiet and you won't come to any harm.'

I did half of what he asked and sat still. My mouth,

however, wasn't so easy to control.

'Where are we going?' I asked. 'Somewhere nice, I hope. With speedboats. And a chocolate waterfall. And … oh, I know what you're going to say. It's—'

'Strictly need to know,' chuckled Brown Cow, as the car sped out of Everyday Avenue. 'And *you* don't need to know.'

4.'HIGHLY-UTTERLY DANGERFYING.'

Exactly nine minutes and forty-seven seconds after we had left Everyday Avenue, the car, that I had regrettably climbed into, came to an abrupt halt.

We had arrived.

Destination unknown.

I caught a whiff of my favourite breakfast cereal as Brown Cow let go of my wrists and exited the car first. I was still licking my lips when he reached back inside, grabbed me by the neck and dragged me out of the vehicle. Before I could get my footing, he had thrown me over his shoulder like a sack of old potatoes. He began to walk and I went with him. A few steps later there was a rise in temperature. At a guess we had moved indoors. There was also a rise in the amount of times my head bounced against the wall, but I chose not to complain. Knowing Brown Cow like I did (not very well at all), he would most probably do it more often if I put the idea in his tiny brain.

'That was … enjoyable,' I moaned, once the biggest of

the goons had plonked me down with an unnecessarily heavy *bump*. 'Now, do you mind removing this thing from my face so I can—'

'Stop speaking,' said Brown Cow bluntly. 'There's something I need to tell you. What you are about to experience will feel quite unusual, but I don't want you to panic. Or scream. Or even wet yourself.'

'Or even wet yourself,' added Grey Hound predictably.

'Dream on,' I laughed. 'There's no way I'll be doing any of ... whoa!'

I yelped in horror as I was lifted off my feet and then turned upside down. Before I knew it, I was just hanging there by my ankles, powerless to fight back.

'I'm going to count to three,' remarked Brown Cow, 'and then I'm going to drop you. Ready?'

'No!' I said hastily. 'Why would I be ready?'

'Three,' began Brown Cow.

'Three,' repeated Grey Hound.

'I said no,' I cried.

'Two,' said Brown Cow.

'Two,' repeated Grey Hound.

'Why are you still counting?' I blurted out. 'I don't want to be dropped. Not now. Not ever. Not—'

Then Brown Cow dropped me.

Suddenly I was falling. No, scratch that. I was actually sliding face-first on my belly. Down, down and then down some more. Despite what they had both said, I still tried to panic, scream and wet myself, but found it almost impossible to do all three things at once. Instead, I held out my hands and waited for the moment of impact. At some point I was going to stop sliding ... and that was the point it was probably going to hurt. Fractured fingers and wonky wrists if I was lucky. And if I wasn't ...

Brace yourself, Hugo.

So I did just that.

Not that I needed to.

My landing, when it arrived, wasn't painful in the slightest. It was actually soft and spongy. And, unless I was mistaken, entirely human.

I had barely caught my breath before two hands swept me into the air and began to carry me like a baby. Twelve steps later the cradling stopped and I was lowered gently to my feet. I was about to speak when Brown Cow beat me to it.

'Sit.'

Placing a heavy hand on my head, he pushed me down until my knees gave way and I collapsed onto the floor.

'Where am I?' I asked nervously.

'You'll find out soon enough,' Brown Cow replied. And he was right. All of a sudden, whatever was on my head was removed and my eyes were back to their best.

The first thing I saw was the top of a writing table. I was sat underneath it, surrounded by empty pizza boxes, one of which Brown Cow had almost certainly used to cover my face in the car.

'Good morning, young Dare. Nice of you to finally pop in.'

I turned to one side and breathed a huge sigh of relief as

I spotted the Big Cheese sat cross-legged beside me. He was the Chief of SICK and, perhaps most incredibly of all, a man who looked more like a walrus (albeit a fully-clothed walrus in a checked suit with matching waistcoat and silk cravat) than an actual walrus itself.

The writing table we were under was the one in the Pantry, the Big Cheese's tiny office. Which also meant that we were in SICK's secret underground headquarters, the SICK Bucket. That explained the sliding. The rubbish chute from The Impossible Pizza takeaway was the only way to enter the premises. It also explained the soft and spongy landing. That was provided by Roland 'Rumble' Robinson. Or rather, his stomach. He was the SICK Bucket's second line of defence and, without doubt, the person who had carried me like a baby from the chute to the Pantry.

'Sorry about the unconventional methods I used to get you here,' boomed the Big Cheese, patting me on the head, 'but I knew Agents Ten and Eleven could be trusted to do the job without too much fuss.'

'Agents Ten and Eleven?' I said, confused. 'Who are they?'

The Big Cheese gestured towards the two men who were stood in the doorway. 'Brown Cow and Grey Hound,' he said proudly. 'I hope it wasn't too much of a shock finding them in your kitchen this morning.'

'It's more of a shock to find out that they're agents for SICK!' I gasped. 'And numbers Ten and Eleven as well. That's generous. I'd hate to meet Twelve and Thirteen—'

'Or even Agent Minus Thirty-Five,' the Big Cheese

frowned. 'I mean, technically you're not even a proper number. Although that's not to say that you're a bad agent. Far from it, in fact. You're just … unusual. And sometimes unusual is exactly what I need. Like today, for instance. So, why don't you thank the two nice agents for bringing you here safely and then we can get down to business?'

I turned up my nose in disgust as I looked out from under the table. 'Thanks for … um … eating my favourite breakfast cereal,' I said, scowling at Brown Cow. My focus shifted to Grey Hound. 'And as for you, thanks for … erm … being stupid enough to slip on that milk,' I muttered.

Both agents nodded their appreciation and then exited the Pantry one small step later, stopping only to close the door behind them.

'You really didn't have to go to all that trouble, sir,' I said, ducking back under the table. 'You could've just asked me. I would've come. After breakfast, of course.'

'I couldn't take that risk, young Dare,' insisted the Big Cheese. 'Not today. There's enough happening already without you going walkabout. Deadly De'Ath is being moved for a start.'

The name alone was enough to get my fingernails in a flap. Despite being stuck in prison, Deadly De'Ath was both the scourge of Crooked Elbow and a criminal genius that everybody seemed to fear. Oh, and he's got a really irritating daughter, but that's another story altogether. No, really, it is. You can read it if you like.

'I hope he's being moved somewhere far away,' I said, crossing my fingers. 'Like a different planet.'

'Almost,' nodded the Big Cheese. 'Deadly De'Ath is actually going up river. Up the River Deep to be precise. He's being transferred from the Crooked Clink to Sol's Solitary Slammer. Not only is it the most isolated prison known to mankind, it's also impossible to escape from. With any luck that's the last we'll ever see of him. He'll be both out of sight and out of mind for the rest of his deadly days.' The Big Cheese stopped suddenly as the smile on his face switched to a grisly grimace. 'Unfortunately, Deadly De'Ath is no longer my number one priority,' he confessed. 'Not now I know what I now know but I didn't know before.'

'Try saying that with your teeth the wrong way round,' I muttered to myself.

'Believe me, young Dare,' the Big Cheese continued, 'what I'm about to tell you is so distressing that we can't afford to waste another second. Or a second after that. Or even a second after that. And definitely not a—'

'Spit it out, sir,' I said, butting in.

The Big Cheese cleared his throat. 'Your mission, young Dare, is like nothing you've ever encountered. It is both highly dangerous and utterly terrifying in equal measures.'

'Highly-utterly dangerfying,' I said, raising an eyebrow. 'But aren't they all?'

'Not like this,' argued the Big Cheese. 'Today is the day when the whole of Crooked Elbow falls foul to the devilish antics of one devious little delinquent.'

'Sounds unpleasant,' I had to admit. 'And I suppose a day like that would have its own name, wouldn't it, sir?'

'Indeed it does.' The Big Cheese began to tremble. 'Today is the Day of the Rascal ... and I'm not coming out from under this table until it's over!'

5.'FROM MISCHIEF TO MURDER.'

The Day of the Rascal.

I waited.

The Big Cheese had said it, but I had no idea what it meant. Judging by the horrified look on his face, however, he must have assumed that I did.

'The Day of the Rascal?' I repeated. 'Is that a bad thing, sir?'

'Is that a bad thing?' The Big Cheese's mouth fell open in disbelief. 'Is ... that ... a ... bad ... thing?'

'That's what I said,' I nodded. 'Would you like me to answer my own question?'

'No, allow me, you witless wally,' the Big Cheese growled. 'Of course the Day of the Rascal is a bad thing. It's the worst thing ever. Worse than stubbing your toe on a table-tennis table. Or trapping your tongue in a trouser press. Or—'

'Missing your mouth completely when you're trying to eat and throwing food over your shoulder,' I chipped in. 'I hate doing that.'

'Codswallop!' barked the Big Cheese. 'Nobody does that. It's not even a *thing*.'

'Yes, it is,' I insisted. 'I once went four whole days without eating because of it. My mother had to follow me around with a dustpan and brush so she could clear up all the mess—'

'Enough!' The Big Cheese pressed a particularly chunky finger to my lips. 'Just … don't. Don't talk. Don't move. Don't even breathe if you can help it. All I want you to do is listen. Then I can tell you what we're faced with—'

'Oh, that's easy, sir,' I said smartly. 'We're faced with each other. I'm looking at you and you're looking at me. It's a bit like a mirror. Except I'm young and handsome and you resemble a bag of onions that's been passed through a washing machine.'

The Big Cheese lifted his hands towards my throat. For a moment I thought he was going to strangle me before he suddenly changed direction and picked up one of the pizza boxes instead. He removed a slice, stopped to think and then removed another.

'You eat and I'll talk,' he instructed, pushing both slices towards my face. 'You've never heard of the Day of The Rascal, have you?'

'Apparently not,' I shrugged. 'Although, if I'm being honest, it's hardly that surprising. Hearing has never been one of my strong points. Not with all that wax I keep wedged inside my ears—'

The Big Cheese pushed the pizza some more until I gave in and opened my mouth. 'I said don't talk. Just nod or shake your head,' he ordered.

So I did. First I nodded. Then I shook my head. Just to prove I could do both.

'Very impressive,' frowned the Big Cheese. 'Right, let's start at the beginning, shall we? No, not the beginning of time – that would be utterly pointless – but the moment we were first aware of the mischief maker behind the Day of the Rascal … and that mischief maker is the Rascal himself! Up until now, he's never been seen—'

'He's never been seen?' I cried between mouthfuls. 'But that means you don't know what he looks like. Come to think of it, how do you even know he's a man?'

'What else could he be?' the Big Cheese laughed.

'A woman,' I replied.

'A woman?' The Big Cheese just stared at me. 'Incredible,' he mumbled. 'Why have I never thought of that?'

'You're very old fashioned, sir,' I said. 'You need to move with the times.'

'I'd rather stay in the past,' the Big Cheese grumbled. 'I was thinner back then. And, believe it or not, a lot younger. Okay, back to your history lesson and it was on this day twenty-seven years ago when things suddenly started to go wrong. First, the Crooked Canal flooded its banks, then all the streetlights exploded, before the wheels fell off every single bus in Crooked Elbow. It was a mystery that nobody could explain. The mystery only intensified, however, when the same kind of things happened a year later on the same day. Trampolines seemed to lose their bounce, the roof blew off the Firework Factory, whilst all the brakes were broken in the cycle shop. The year after that and it happened again. And then again the year after that. And again. And again. And again. And … would you like me to go on, young Dare?'

'I think I've heard enough, sir,' I said. 'It all sounds rather unfortunate, but accidents do happen.'

'Indeed … just not on the same day of every single year,' argued the Big Cheese. 'No, this was the work of the Rascal. We know that because he always leaves a paper scroll at the scene of every crime confessing to his misdemeanours.'

'That's very honest of him,' I remarked.

'Or just big-headed,' said the Big Cheese. 'To be brutally honest, young Dare, I've never really paid much attention to his perilous pranks in the past. Yes, the Rascal has always been a sneaky little sausage, but nowhere near sneaky enough to worry SICK. These were things the Crooked Constabulary could deal with. Nothing too serious. Nothing life-threatening. Until … this year.' The Big Cheese took a breath to compose himself. 'This year the Rascal has upped the ante,' he said anxiously. 'He's gone to a whole new level of naughtiness. To put it bluntly, he's going to … kill me!'

'You?' I blurted out. 'That's a big jump, sir, from mischief to murder. Why would he possibly want to kill you?'

'I am rather important, you know,' insisted the Big Cheese. 'I'm the Chief of SICK. Crooked Elbow's number one spymaster. Take a look at this if you still need convincing …' Reaching inside the pocket of his jacket, the Big Cheese removed a paper scroll. 'You *can* read, can't you?' he asked, passing it to me.

'What do you think?' I unrolled the scroll and read it quickly before he could answer. Then I read it again because I felt under pressure the first time and missed out a few words. It was short and not particularly sweet. Oh, what's that? You'd like me to share it with you? As you wish …

Dear Mr Cheese,

The Day of the Rascal will be your last day on this planet. Hope you don't mind.

Lots of love and wet kisses, the Rascal.

'Strange,' I frowned, 'but it doesn't actually say anywhere that you're going to die.'

'That's what I thought, too.' The Big Cheese handed me another scroll. 'And then I got this …'

Dear Mr Cheese,

In case you're wondering, that means you're going to die. Sorry for any misunderstanding. No offence intended.

Take care, the Rascal.

'Okay, that does kind of spell it out,' I admitted, 'but it still doesn't say anywhere that the Rascal is going to kill you … oh, you haven't!'

'I have.' The Big Cheese passed me another scroll. It was identical to the other two in all but one way. This one really *did* spell it out. In words that even I could understand.

Dear Mr Cheese,

This is awkward. When I said that you were going to die, what I actually meant was that I was going to kill you. I should really try and explain myself more clearly in future.

See you soon, the Rascal.

'That's not all.' The Big Cheese removed a bulging pile of scrolls from inside his jacket and waved them in my face. 'There are hundreds of them,' he sighed. 'Well, at least thirty-three. But they all say the same thing. That, one way or another, I'm going to die. And it's to happen today. On the Day of the Rascal.' The Big Cheese stopped suddenly and winked at me. 'Except it's not.'

'It's not?' I repeated. 'That's good news … for you.'

'It's good news for both of us,' insisted the Big Cheese. 'I've got every single agent out searching for the Rascal, but there's only one spy who I really trust to keep me alive.'

'And you'd like me to go and fetch them for you, sir?' I offered.

'No, you are *them*, you blithering bunion,' barked the Big Cheese. 'That's why I dragged you from your house at stupid o'clock this morning. You, young Dare, are going to stop the Rascal.'

'Me?' At the same time I snatched another slice of pizza just in case it was the last thing I ever ate. 'Why me, sir?' I wondered. 'Why not Brown Cow or Grey Hound or any of the other agents who come before Minus Thirty-Five in the pecking order?'

'You know why, young Dare,' remarked the Big Cheese. 'You're one of a kind. A freak of nature. Whether it's deliberate or not, you have skills that no one else has ever attempted to learn. For starters, you're not afraid of looking foolish. And you do. Often. And you're brave as well. Or just bonkers. Either way, even in your slippers you dare to go where others fear to tread. And best of all no one ever sees you coming. You're hidden in plain sight. Disguised without the disguise. They just think you're another spotty, smelly schoolboy. Which you are, of course, but you're also something else. You're a spy. No, you're *my* spy.'

I screwed up my face. 'Thank you, sir, for your … erm … interesting choice of words. Okay, I think I get it now. It's quite simple really. You want me to risk my neck to save yours.'

'Precisely.' The Big Cheese glanced at his watch. 'By the time you leave the SICK Bucket it'll be six o'clock in the morning. That leaves eighteen hours in the day. Eighteen hours for you to take out the Rascal before the Rascal takes out me.'

'And what will you be doing, sir?' I asked.

'I'll be under this table,' the Big Cheese revealed. 'With the lights off and my eyes closed. Oh, and with more pizza than one large man can possibly handle. Perfectly safe.'

'You hope,' I muttered to myself. 'So, where do you want me to start? How do I catch someone who has never been seen?'

'I thought you might ask me that.' The Big Cheese fell silent. For quite a long time actually. Almost a minute. 'Truth is, I don't know,' he admitted eventually. 'I haven't got a clue. I mean, there is one slight lead, but I don't know how reliable it is. There's a house on the spooky side of

Crooked Elbow called Hag's Hole. Now, I'm not one to start rumours, but it's supposed to be haunted by the ghost of the old lady who used to live there. Her name was Hettie the Hag, but … why have you gone so pale, young Dare?'

'Why do you think?' I moaned. 'Haunted houses? Hag's Hole? Hettie the Hag? I'm a spy, not a ghost hunter. Would you go there, sir, if somebody asked you to?'

'That would never happen,' mumbled the Big Cheese sheepishly. 'Just try and put that ghostly gobbledygook to one side and listen. The whispers I've heard amongst the undesirables suggest that the Rascal has been hiding out in Hag's Hole for the past year or so. Don't look so nervous, young Dare. I'm not sending you in alone. Violet Crow will meet you at the garden gate and hold your hand if you ask politely.'

'Violet Crow, sir?' I said.

'Agent Sixteen,' explained the Big Cheese. 'One of the finest spies I have at my disposal. And also an expert in disguise. Crow could be dressed as anything when you meet. A window cleaner … a bus driver … even a door. Talking of which, let me introduce you to the one behind you. You can take a closer look on your way out …'

'Message received loud and clear, sir.' I tried to stand, but forgot where I was and bumped my head on the table. 'Ouch!'

'Be careful,' groaned the Big Cheese. 'This is my home for the rest of the day and I don't want it getting destroyed. If I'm being honest, I don't want you getting destroyed either. This, however, should help you stay alive for the foreseeable …'

I was still rubbing my head when I bent down and looked back under the table. The Big Cheese was holding something long and thin with a curved end.

'If that's a walking stick then I don't think I need it,' I insisted.

'Well, I think you do,' disagreed the Big Cheese. 'Not only is it a useful weapon in times of crisis, but it's also extendable. And when I say extendable, I'm talking *spectacularly* extendable. It was your father who invented it—'

'You mean Dirk Dare, the greatest spy who never was,' I said proudly.

'You don't have to say that every time I mention him,' sighed the Big Cheese. 'But, yes, your father invented it and gave it to me for my birthday. It's not that I'm ungrateful, young Dare, but, as you know, gadgets and I don't really get along.'

'I feel the same way about soap, sir,' I said. 'And mothballs. And barbed wire. And—'

'You can go now,' remarked the Big Cheese bluntly.

I accepted the walking stick and made my way towards the exit. 'And manhole covers. And sardines. And—'

'Goodbye,' hollered the Big Cheese. 'Close the door on your way out.'

I did as he asked, but not before pausing to glance up at the clock right outside the Pantry. The Big Cheese was right. It was six o'clock in the morning. There were eighteen hours left in the day.

Eighteen hours to track down the Rascal.

First stop Hag's Hole.

I'll meet you there.

6.'IT'S BETTER TO BE SAFE THAN SORRY.'

You took your time.

Don't fret; I won't hold it against you. I'm not that kind of spy. Instead, I'll tell you everything I've learnt whilst I've been waiting for you to arrive.

On first inspection, Hag's Hole was pretty grim.

No, scratch that. In actual fact it was a *lot* grim. With added grimness. And a sprinkling of grimbles for good measure.

A tall, twisted building, it had been built to a gothic style before being plonked slap-bang in the middle of nowhere (although probably not in that order). It had taken me over an hour to get there after leaving the Pantry, but then twenty-one minutes of that I had spent hunting for a map of Crooked Elbow in the bowels of the SICK Bucket (that's the filing cabinet to you and me) and another seventeen changing into the Big Cheese's spare set of clothing. Now I was dressed in checked trousers with an identical waistcoat, white shirt, silk cravat and suede loafers. All of them were at least five sizes too big for me, but I couldn't go out in search of the Rascal in nothing but my pyjamas (been there, done that, never again).

Back to Hag's Hole, and the most haunted house in Crooked Elbow (copyright Hugo Dare) had arched windows, a shabby-looking dome-shaped door and a tall, steeple-like tower, all of which only added to its seriously spooky demeanour. As did the smoke that was rising from the chimney. Either the house was on fire or someone had deliberately lit one in the fireplace. The Rascal perhaps. That would make my day at least forty-eight times easier if it was. With any luck, I could even be home before breakfast.

No, *we* could be home before breakfast.

I wasn't alone in this. I had found the garden gate with its peeling paint and creaking hinges, but now I had to find Agent Sixteen.

Codename Violet Crow.

Right on cue I caught a flash of something fluorescent moving at speed towards me. I squinted into the darkness, took a chance and guessed it was a man.

A man in colourful clothing and matching headband.

A man in colourful clothing and matching headband who just happened to be jogging along the pavement.

A jogger then. Obviously. Let's hope it doesn't take me so long to explain things in the future (that's if we both make it that far, of course).

I started to wonder if this was Violet Crow. The Big Cheese had said they were an expert when it came to disguises, and jogger was as good a disguise as any.

Ever the gentleman, I was about to step forward and introduce myself when something unexpected leapt over the garden gate and landed beside me. No, not something. This was more like a someone.

A woman, in fact.

Dressed entirely in black, she had short, spiky hair, sharp eyes, a particularly pointy chin and one long monobrow that took up much of her forehead. At a guess she was older than me, but younger than my mother (anywhere between fourteen and eighty then. No, my mistake. Doreen's not that old. More like seventy-nine. And a half.)

The jogger hesitated. Bad move. Racing across the pavement, Spiky hit him head-on and the two of them tumbled to the ground.

I had seen enough. In one swift motion, I removed the walking stick that the Big Cheese had given me from my over-sized trousers and gave it a good, hard flick. To my surprise, the stick extended (and then extended some more) before eventually prodding Spiky in the back of the head.

'Do that again and I'll snap it in half!' she scowled.

I flinched as she turned towards me. She had one of those faces. The kind that made you run away and ask questions later. Much later. So late, in fact, that there was no chance that she'd even hear you.

'Put down that walking stick and do exactly what I tell you,' hissed Spiky. 'I've got a gag in my pocket. And some cable ties. Get them for me … now!'

I didn't. Instead, I just stood there, unsure of my next move.

'Oh, it's like that, is it?' Spiky kept an evil eye on me as she removed the gag herself and stuffed it into the jogger's mouth. 'You're a long way from home, little boy. What are you doing here?'

'No, what are *you* doing here?' I cried. 'And why do you feel the need to squash that poor man's face into the concrete?'

'You can never be too careful,' replied Spiky. 'Who knows who might be lurking about in the darkness. Especially today of all days.'

And then it clicked into place.

'The Day of the Rascal,' I said, nodding to myself. 'You're Violet Crow, aren't you?'

'If you say so,' muttered Spiky. The jogger struggled beneath her, but not enough to prevent the woman I now knew to be Agent Sixteen from fastening the cable ties around his wrists and ankles.

'Yes, I say so,' I insisted. 'I don't want to give you a swollen head, but what you just did was quite impressive. Maybe you could teach me some moves when you've got time. Although, if I'm being honest, I'm not overly fond of your disguise. All in black is so predictable for a spy. I prefer the jogger look,' I said, gesturing towards the man who was now gagged and bound on the pavement. 'Is he the Rascal?'

'How am I supposed to know?' shrugged Crow.

'But you knocked him over?' I said, confused. 'Why would you do that if you didn't know who he was?'

'It's better to be safe than sorry,' said Crow matter-of-factly. At the same time, she hopped up onto her feet. Fearful for my safety, I took a step back, just in case she decided to pounce on me like she had the jogger.

Fortunately, she didn't.

She did, however, grab me in a headlock.

'Too slow, little boy,' growled Crow. 'You know all about me, so now it's your turn. Who are you?'

'Not who ... Hugo,' I said, gasping for breath. 'Hugo Dare. You were sent here to meet me—'

'And now we *have* met,' Crow frowned, 'and it wasn't all that interesting. So, who sent you? You're too small and weedy to be here spying—'

'That's what you think,' I said smugly.

'You're a spy?' Violet Crow slowly shook her head. 'Unbelievable. Who do you work for? Surely SICK wouldn't sink so low as to—'

'I think you'll find they would,' I said with added smugness. 'I'm Agent Minus Thirty-Five. Codename Pink Weasel.'

'You're the spy they've sent to catch the Rascal?' Violet Crow kept on shaking her head as she tightened her grip. 'That's disappointing,' she grumbled. 'I expected more from the Big Cheese. Maybe he doesn't take the Rascal's threats seriously.'

'Oh, he takes them very seriously,' I argued. 'That's why he's got every agent out searching Crooked Elbow whilst he hides under the table in the Pantry. He's so worried, in fact, that Deadly De'Ath's trip up the River Deep to Sol's Solitary Slammer is no longer his chief concern.'

Violet Crow raised her one long monobrow. 'He might regret that later in the day.'

'Not if he's still alive he won't.' I nodded towards the house. 'Are we going in there together?' I asked. 'Safety in numbers. Oldest first and prettiest second. You at the front and me right behind, looking over your shoulder. You know it makes sense.'

'I'm not going anywhere with you,' replied Crow bluntly. 'I don't work as a team. It's nothing personal. I just don't like people … and people don't like me.'

'I can see how that might be the case,' I muttered. 'You are a little … hands on, after all. Talking of which …'

Violet Crow seemed to get the hint as she finally released her grip and I slipped out from under her armpit.

'You go your way, Weasel, and I'll go mine,' she remarked. It was more an order than an observation. 'First, I'm going to deal with this repulsive runner and then I'm going to do what everybody else is doing. I'm going to look for the Rascal … but, unlike the rest of you simple-minded spies, I'm going to find him!'

I didn't disagree. Why would I? If Violet Crow wanted to get the job done then that was fine by me. If nothing else, it saved me from having to do it.

'What about Hag's Hole?' I asked.

'What about it?' snapped Crow, as she hauled the jogger up off the pavement. 'It's completely empty. Any fool can see that. You won't find the Rascal in there.'

She had a point. It did look empty. Looks, however, can be deceptive …

'I'm going to check anyway,' I insisted. 'Just to be sure.'

'You do that,' snorted Crow. Turning sharply, she stuck

a hand under the jogger's waistband and began to drag him along the pavement by his shorts. 'Be seeing you, Weasel ...'

I waved as she crossed the road and disappeared into the darkness. Unsurprisingly, Crow didn't wave back.

With my route to Hag's Hole no longer obstructed by either suspicious joggers or flying agents, I pulled open the gate and made my way along the winding path towards the house. The grass in the garden had died a long time ago and nothing very floral seemed to be growing in the flower beds.

There was a huge brass knocker in the centre of the door. I banged on it twice and then stepped back.

Twenty-four ... twenty-five ... twenty-six seconds later and nobody had come to answer. By the twenty-seventh I had crouched down, opened the letterbox and peered inside. An icy blast attacked my eyeballs immediately, forcing me to blink away the tears before I could look again. Despite the murky interior, I could just about make out a light coming from somewhere along the hallway. A bulb perhaps. Or a torch.

No, it was a candle.

I only realised that when the flame danced and flickered, but never seemed to go out. I blinked once more and saw that the candle was drawing closer to the door. When I blinked again it was so close I could feel the heat coming through the letterbox.

I looked away before it singed my eyelashes. The letterbox rattled, but in the silence that followed I thought I could hear, first, footsteps and then a voice coming from inside. It was barely a whisper.

I took a second or four to try and compose myself. Not only was my mind running wild, but now every other part of my body had decided to join it. That wasn't like me at all. I was a spy. I didn't get scared. Not often, anyway. Only on bath day.

I steadied my nerves and lifted the letterbox, ready to look again. Maybe it was just my imagination. No footsteps. No voice. And definitely nothing to be afraid of.

The candle seemed to have vanished, but now something else had replaced it.

No, make that two things.

Wide and unblinking, there was a pair of eyes staring straight back at me.

I held their stare until the letterbox slammed shut. I was about to open it again when something fell out. I caught it before it landed and held it up to the street light. It was a slip of paper.

A slip of paper with four words printed on one side in black crayon.

ENTERS IF YOU DARE

7.'THINGS ARE NEVER AS BAD AS THEY SEEM.'

I rolled the slip of paper into a ball and stuck it in my mouth.

Then I took it out again and put it in my pocket.

My plan was to swallow it, but it was bigger than I expected. Totally inedible, in fact. Forget that, though, because it's not important. Not anymore. Not now I knew there was somebody inside Hag's Hole. Somebody who had invited me to join them. But only if I dared.

If *I* dared? Me? Of course I dared. How could I not?

Dare by name and dare by nature.

Clambering to my feet, I chose the easy option and yanked on the door handle. It didn't move. The door was locked. Not so easy, after all.

Moving cautiously around the side of the house, I passed two windows that were both stained with dirt and covered in cobwebs, and then another that was boarded up with cardboard. It was only when I turned the corner that I found what I was looking for.

The back door.

I didn't try the handle – no one likes to be foiled the same way twice in quick succession – but concentrated, instead, on something slightly lower down.

The cat-flap.

It seemed larger than usual, but then I'd never been face-to-flap with one before so I was hardly an expert. My first move was to poke my head through the square-shaped opening. It was worryingly gloomy inside Hag's Hole, but that wasn't enough to stop me from spying something small and furry scampering across the floor. It wasn't big enough to be the cat that fitted the flap and probably not as friendly either. A rat then. Just what I didn't need.

I had two options and neither of them exactly appealed.

I could either get in or get out.

I watched as the rat scurried away and decided there was no reason for me to do the same thing.

Some people would have thought it beyond the realms of possibility for a thirteen-year-old boy to squeeze through a cat flap, but that wasn't true. It was just hard. Really hard. Like *scrape my shoulders, rub my ribs and practically erase my elbows* hard. Definitely not impossible, though.

I was in.

Scrambling up off the filthy floor, I steered towards the nearest wall in search of a light switch. Somewhat predictably, the nearest wall was the worst wall I could've chosen and I almost fell into what appeared to be a sink. The taps were bone dry as if they hadn't been turned on in years, whilst a strange, plant-like creation had started to sprout out of the plughole. I kept on moving, using the work surfaces to guide me. All of them were covered in a thick layer of dust. As was the kettle. And the toaster. At least I knew where I was now – in the kitchen – although any hopes I had of stumbling upon a spot of breakfast seemed highly unlikely under the circumstances.

I mean, there was always the rat droppings if I was really desperate …

Don't go there, Hugo.

I put all thoughts of food to the back of my mind as I set off blindly for the opposite side of the room. Five steps later I found it, albeit with my nose. If only I had lifted my hands to soften the impact. Obvious really. Still, no point crying over swollen nostrils. It only hurt a little. Honestly.

Several minutes later the blood had stopped flowing and I could get back to searching for the light switch. I eventually found it, but nothing happened when I flicked it on. Great. After all that fuss, the light didn't even work.

Now I was really confused. Hag's Hole seemed to be completely uninhabited and yet there was no doubt I had seen a pair of eyes in the letterbox. And eyes like that definitely didn't belong to a ghost.

A noise above my head confused things further. The floorboards were creaking. Yes, it does happen from time to time, but this was more than that. This sounded as if there was somebody on the move upstairs. Shuffling over to the kitchen door, I slowly eased it open and made my way into the hallway, unsure what I would find …

Oh, not very much as it turns out.

The hallway, just like the kitchen, was shrouded in

darkness with its own equal measures of dust across every surface and a fair amount of scurrying that I tried desperately to ignore. If I looked hard enough I could see the door that I had earlier knocked on straight ahead of me, not to mention the letterbox that I had peered through.

And next to it, a staircase.

Wary of treading on anything that might *squeak*, I crept towards the latter as carefully as possible. It was only when I kicked the bottom step that I realised I wasn't careful enough. I held my breath as the noise echoed out around Hag's Hole, and then held it some more whilst I waited to see if anyone appeared on the floor above. They didn't, so I set off up the stairs. Every step made its own high-pitched, whining sound. Or maybe that was just me. Through no fault of my own I was producing noises from both top and bottom. Don't look at me like that. It's not my fault. I was just nervous, that's all.

Nervous about what could jump out at me at any moment.

This was the most haunted house in Crooked Elbow (copyright Hugo Dare) … and I had a bad feeling I was about to find out why.

My knees were knocking and I could barely stand by the time I reached the top of the staircase. There were two doors in front of me, both of which were closed. Behind the door to my left, however, I could hear a peculiar tapping sound. Footsteps perhaps. With that in mind, I chose left over right and tip-toed towards it.

Four tip-toes later, I stopped. There was a sign swinging from the door. Like the slip of paper in the letterbox, it was written in black crayon.

STAYS OUT OR ELSE!

The message was both simple to understand and impossible to ignore. And if that was the case, then so be it. As you wish. Give me a minute and I'll meet you outside …

'Get a grip, Hugo,' I muttered under my breath. 'Things are never as bad as they seem.'

Taking my own advice, I crossed my arms and grabbed hold of my waist to stop myself from shaking. I could do this. And, even if I couldn't, I was still going to try.

As every good spy knows, the only way to enter a room you're not supposed to is in a fast and furious manner. Wade in without warning. Ready and raring to go. That way you can catch whoever happens to be in there off-guard.

At least, that was what I kept trying to convince myself.

Fumbling for the handle, I burst into the room and kept on moving. I couldn't see a thing, but that was only to be expected.

Unlike what happened next.

I took two steps forward and my stomach leapt up into my throat. To my horror there was nothing beneath my feet. And if there was nothing beneath my feet, there was only one possible outcome.

I was going to drop.

And guess what? I did.

8.'DIDN'T YOU SPOTTY THE SIGN?'

My natural reaction was to reach out and grab something.

I tried to do just that, shocked to find that it actually worked. Whatever I had grabbed hold of was strong enough to take my weight. Now I was no longer falling; I was just stranded. Everything below my waist was swinging back and forth, whilst the rest of me was balanced precariously on some kind of ledge. One wrong move and ...

'Help!' With my grip weakening and my fingers beginning to slip, I couldn't afford to be picky about who heard me. 'Someone! Anyone! Help!'

Hanging there in mid-air was rapidly becoming something I could only dream of.

The nightmare, meanwhile, was that I couldn't hold on at all.

'Didn't you spotty the sign?'

I heard the voice at the same time as the room was illuminated. The first thing I noticed was how little of me was actually visible above the floorboards.

The second was the frail old lady who was stood in the doorway.

Her face was as wrinkled as a sunbathing walnut, whilst her eyes were brighter than the same sun that had wrinkled the walnut to begin with. Like candyfloss on a windy day, her hair was both white in colour and incredibly fluffy. As were her eyebrows. And her clothes, although they appeared to have picked up a number of stains along the way. Red and yellow and pink and blue were all fighting for space on some kind of over-sized smock. All the colours of the rainbow, in fact. Definitely not something you'd expect a rotter like the Rascal to wear. Or your average ghost for that matter.

'Didn't you spotty the sign?' the rainbow lady repeated. 'Clear as a muddy puddle it most certainly is not. Simple-pimple. Stays out or else.'

'Yes, I spotty it ... I mean, *saw* it,' I gasped. 'Now, is there any way you can help me out of here?'

'Possibly not possible,' the rainbow lady shrugged. 'Heart says yep, but age says nope. Have had a dinky thinky thought, though. That thingamajig poking out your trousers should do the tricksy. Passes it here, please and thank you.'

'I beg your ... oh, I see.' I let go with one hand so I could remove the walking stick from where I had hidden it. One quick flick later and the stick began to extend.

Grabbing the curved end before it hit her in the face, the rainbow lady glanced around the room before deciding to hook it over the door handle. To my surprise it seemed to hold firm. That was my cue to start scrambling upwards like my life depended on it. It wasn't until I had rolled to safety, however, that I finally got to take a look at what I had actually fallen through. This was far worse than just a crack in the wood. No, as far as I could tell, the floorboards had completely rotted away, leaving a hole so large that, if I had failed to hang on, I would've dropped all the way down to the ground floor. Haunted house or not, that was simply unacceptable. Surely there should have been some sort of notice up to warn people of the dangers. A sign perhaps. On the door.

Oh, this is awkward …

'So, do you read or do read you not?' asked the rainbow lady confusingly.

I sat up and caught my breath. My hands were stinging a little, but, other than that, I seemed to have escaped unharmed. 'You're not the first person to ask me that today,' I replied.

'So, spotty the sign, reads the sign, but wanders in regardless,' muttered the rainbow lady, slowly shaking her candyfloss. 'Struggling to see the sensicals in that, I am.'

'You're not the only one,' I had to admit. 'Truth is, I wasn't paying attention. I was too busy searching for the Rascal—'

'The Rascal?' The rainbow lady shivered on the spot. 'If that's the case then you've come to the right placey-plops.'

'The right … place?' I said, struggling to decipher her own unique way of talking. 'But that means … no, not you! *You* can't be the Rascal?'

'No, I can't,' agreed the rainbow lady. 'Not the Rascal … but I am a Hettie.'

'Hettie the Hag?' I looked her up and down, but resisted the urge to reach out and touch her to see if she was a ghost. 'I thought you were ... you know ... not here anymore ... somewhere else entirely ... in the land of the not-so-living.' I was mumbling and I didn't like it. 'You're supposed to be dead,' I said bluntly. 'Although clearly you're not. Even I can see that ... I think. I mean ... maybe I should check ... you're not dead, are you?'

'Definitely a no-no,' insisted Hettie. 'Even if some foul and frightful folk were wishing that I was.'

I screwed up my face. 'Sorry ... I wasn't trying to be ... not intentionally anyway—'

'Forget it forgotten,' said Hettie, waving my apology away as she helped me to my feet. 'Henrietta Hagglethorpe is the name I was beginning with, but that was far and away too muchly of a mouthful for most around here to spit out. They turned Henrietta into Hettie and Hettie into Hettie the Hag. Just rudey, that was. Not as rudey as when they all said I had dropped off the planet and died the dreaded death, mind. Because I haven't. Still here, I am.'

'I can certainly vouch for that,' I nodded.

Hettie took a moment to study my walking stick before finally handing it back to me. 'What are you exactly?' she asked, out of the blue. 'Certainly not ordinary because ordinary don't come peeking-and-a-poking round Hag's Hole. Too spooked, they are. Spooked about the ghosties and the ghoulies. Ha, what a chuckle that is!' Hettie laughed once and then stopped to draw a long, wheezing breath. 'No, more like a slug in a snowstorm you are,' she remarked.

'Differently different. And maybe just a little bitty bit special.'

'Special like a spy,' I said smoothly. I took a second or two to think of something equally as smart to follow that up with. It was no surprise, however, when my mind drew a blank. 'Because that's what I am,' I mumbled eventually. 'A spy. Codename Pink Weasel. But you can call me—'

'Weaselly,' guessed Hettie.

I nodded. 'Yeah, that'll do.'

'No, *you'll* do,' insisted Hettie. 'Given up hope, I had, that any human bodies would ever come-a-calling, but then I hear you, knock-knock-knocking on Hettie's door, wanting to come right on in. How you did, though, baffles my brain ...'

'Cat flap,' I revealed.

'Oh, ever so cleverly clever that is,' grinned Hettie. 'My cat, Pudding, never could say no to a munchie. He was a big old boy, make no mistakers.'

'Was?' I repeated. 'Is Pudding no longer with us?'

'No, not with us,' replied Hettie sadly. She swallowed before she spoke again. 'Downstairs, he is. Itching in the kitchen. But back in the day, he was hugely humongous. Like three cats in one skin. Tight squeeze, if you please. Had to widen his cat flap, so I did. Oh, the shame on my face. Two days and a week later he started his diet ... his choice, mine not ... and now he's thinner than a thin thing. More like a rat than a cat. Surprised you didn't spotty him when you wriggled and jiggled your way into Hag's Hole.'

'Maybe I did,' I said, remembering the small and furry

creature I had seen scurrying about the kitchen. 'Still, if it wasn't for Pudding I would never have got in to begin with. And if it wasn't for you I would never have climbed out of those floorboards. Not unless the Rascal decided to come and help me.'

'The Rascal? Not on your nostrils!' said Hettie fiercely. 'Rather watch you drop to your gloomy-doom than race at pace to your rescue, he would. Ask him yourself if believe me you don't.' Hettie pointed towards the ceiling. 'The Rascal's up, up, up and away,' she revealed. 'He's in the tower … and I know just the Weaselly who can get him out of there.'

9.'BYE-BYES FOR NOW-NOW.'

Hettie took me by the hand and guided me away from the hole in the floorboards.

I think she was worried about me falling through for a second time. And, knowing me like I did, she had a right to be.

'So, you've seen him then?' I asked. 'The Rascal?'

'Not with my own peepers, I haven't,' admitted Hettie.

Oh dear. 'Then how do you know he's a man?'

Hettie took a moment to think. 'What else could he be?'

I rolled my eyes when I was sure she wasn't watching. I had been here before. Not in Hag's Hole, but in this conversation. Back in the SICK Bucket with the Big Cheese. 'The Rascal could always be a … woman,' I explained.

'A woman?' laughed Hettie. 'A woman like me?'

'Not necessarily,' I replied. 'There are plenty of other women out there. Taller … shorter … younger … older … no, probably not older—'

'A man is the Rascal,' said Hettie stubbornly. 'Sure of it, I am. Sixty-three per-cent certain. Nearly sixty-four.'

'That's reassuring,' I moaned. 'Are you sixty-three per

cent certain – nearly sixty-four – that he's up in the tower, too?' I asked, striking the ceiling with my walking stick.

'Don't be doing that!' Without warning, Hettie ushered me straight out the door and into the only other room on the first floor. There was a small bed in there, as well as a fireplace that was still smouldering and a small wooden rocking chair. It was the last of these (and definitely not the fire) which Hettie promptly sat on. 'Can do our talking time in here,' she whispered. 'No more whacking on the ceiling, though. Because if the Rascal hears, then the Rascal escapes. And if the Rascal escapes, then they'll be no catchy-catching him. And if there's no catchy-catching him, then the whole of Crooked Elbow will suffer insufferably. Forever and ever and after that as well. And we all know whose fault *that* would be.'

'Bit drastic,' I frowned.

'Not drasticals enough,' insisted Hettie. 'The Rascal is a slippery, slimy snake, make no mistakers.'

'And yet you still let him live in your house,' I said, confused.

'I don't let him; I need him,' said Hettie, correcting me. 'The Rascal is my lodger. Bills don't pay themselves, worse luck. I mean, I did think it a little oddly strange when he refused to meet and greet or talk and speak, but then he gave me three months' rent upfront so I could hardly grumble. Left scrolls all over the house for me as well, he did. Lots and lots of those pesky rolling scrolls. Back and forth and back again. Told me what to do and when to do it. At the end of the day, I just thought he was a particularly private human body … that is, until I found out who he really was.'

'What gave him away?' I wondered.

'The sign on his door,' revealed Hettie. '*The Rascal's Bedroom.* Wandered up there once, I did … then wandered straight back down again. Wouldn't go anywhere near there today, tomorrow or next Thursday even if you paid me. Everybody and anybody knows that crossing coattails with the Rascal brings nothing but bad luck and plenty of it.'

'Everybody and anybody … except me,' I said. 'I don't believe in bad luck. Or good luck. Or even that middling luck. You know the kind; a combination of the two. Like if you trip over your own shoelaces, but then land face-first in a tub of ice-cream.'

'Funny that,' muttered Hettie under her breath. 'Would've thought someone with a freaky face like yours would've believed in bad luck.'

Unsure whether or not that was a compliment or an insult, I gave my crumbly new friend both the benefit of the doubt and half a smile as I opened the door and stepped out onto the landing. The coast was clear so I cautiously made my way towards the staircase that led all the way up to the tower. The first step groaned in despair the moment I placed my weight on it.

'Bye-byes for now-now,' whispered Hettie from the doorway. 'See you on the other side.'

I waited until she had closed the door before I continued up the stairs. The higher I climbed, the darker it seemed to get. So much so, in fact, that by the time I had reached the top step I may as well have had my eyes closed.

Oh, my mistake. I *did* have my eyes closed. I wouldn't have thought that was possible without me realising.

It was still dark when I opened them, but not dark enough to stop me from noticing the outline of a door directly in front of me. Creeping towards it, I instantly spotted the sign that confirmed everything Hettie had told me.

The Rascal's Bedroom

I tried to put all thoughts of gaping holes and broken floorboards to the back of my mind as I knocked twice, waited for less than a second and then burst into the room with all guns blazing. Well, I was swinging a walking stick above my head. That was close enough for me.

If the Rascal was in his bedroom then he wouldn't know what had hit him.

At least, that was what I hoped.

Turns out I was wrong, though.

Horribly wrong …

10.'I DON'T SCARE EASILY.'

I stopped swinging the walking stick the moment I set foot in the Rascal's Bedroom.

I stopped doing everything, in fact. Moving. Breathing. Dancing (no, scratch that. A spy like me never dances. Not even if my armpits are on fire.)

To be honest, there was a good reason why I had come to a sudden standstill. A better than good reason.

A *gun* reason.

Not only was it the first thing I saw as I charged into the Rascal's empty bedroom, but it was also pointing straight at me. I looked beyond the gun's barrel and spotted the outline of a figure. Tucked away in the far corner of the room, hidden in the shadows, the figure's size and shape seemed to suggest it was a man.

A man who had to be the Rascal.

He was dressed in a dark coat that reached all the way down to his feet and a trilby hat that was pulled so low it covered much of his face. The gun was resting in his right hand whilst something long and thin was poking out of his mouth. A cigar perhaps, although it didn't appear to be lit.

Stood rooted to the spot, fixed with fear, all I could do was wait for the inevitable moment that the Rascal pulled the trigger.

Nine seconds later and I was still waiting.

Another nine after that and the waiting game showed no sign of coming to an end.

I began to count again, but failed to get past three. If the Rascal was going to shoot he probably would've done it by now. Which meant that maybe I had a chance. Just a squeak. A sliver. A slice. Still, any chance is better than no chance at all …

'Whoops! Wrong room,' I remarked. 'I was looking for the … the … the lavatory.' As excuses went, it was as good as any (even if it was complete and utter nonsense). 'Now, I don't mean to put a dampener on things, but there's a strong possibility I could wet myself at any given moment. Worst case scenario, it'll run all the way down the leg of my trousers before dripping out the bottom. You'll probably have to go and fetch a mop and bucket to clean up the mess. So, with that in mind … if it's alright with you … I think I'll just …'

I started to shuffle backwards. One way or another, the Rascal would have to react. Maybe shout or scream or spring into action. Or just shoot. No, not shoot! Why would I say that?

In the end, I needn't have worried because he didn't do any of those things.

Although that was largely because he didn't do anything. Which, if you ask me, was very strange behaviour indeed.

Heading back into the room, I did the unthinkable and

marched straight up to the man I believed to be the Rascal. I came to a halt when we were eyeball to eyeball. Except we weren't. Because he didn't have any. Eyeballs, I mean. Or eyelashes. Or even eyebrows. Whilst we're at it, he didn't have a nose or a mouth or ears or any other facial features I could think of. And I didn't expect to find much under that coat either. Because this wasn't the Rascal.

It was just a shop window dummy.

A shop window dummy that wasn't even carrying a gun. No, it was a water pistol. Which meant that even if the Rascal had fired, the worst that would've happened to me was a good soaking as opposed to a bullet hole in my belly.

Last but not least, I looked again at what was sticking out of the dummy's mouth. Like everything else in the room, I had wrongly identified it as a cigar. It was actually a paper scroll.

A paper scroll that was identical to the ones that the Big Cheese had shown me in the SICK Bucket.

I carefully removed it from its resting place so I could read what had been written inside.

> *To the spy who seeks me,*
>
> *The Day of the Rascal has begun. This is your thirteen second warning. Leave Hag's Hole immediately … or else! If you do manage to get out alive then make your way to Mysterious Melvin's Museum of Mind-Bending Marvels. Don't be late … because I won't wait.*
>
> *Kind regards, the Rascal.*

I slotted the scroll back where I had found it. I didn't really take the warning seriously, but began the countdown nevertheless.

Thirteen. Twelve. Eleven …

If everything I had read was true, then Hettie was right. Even if the Rascal wasn't in his bedroom now, he had been there at some point. He had even gone as far as to set a trap with the dummy and the water pistol for someone to walk straight into. Someone who was hot on his heels. Someone who was closing in on him with every passing second.

Someone like me.

Ten. Nine. Eight …

It was time to leave. Thankfully, I didn't have to think too hard about my next destination.

Mysterious Melvin's Museum of Mind-Bending Marvels.

I had only been there once before, but it had certainly left a lasting impression. Both weird and wonderful in equal measures (but then the same could be said about yours truly), it was home to all manner of things that should never really have been created, but, now they had, were actually quite fascinating.

Seven. Six. Five …

The thing I couldn't understand, however, was why the Rascal had demanded that I get out of Hag's Hole in thirteen seconds. And, perhaps more importantly, what would happen to me if I didn't?

Four. Three. Two. One …

The countdown was complete.

'Nice try,' I said, patting the dummy on the cheek. 'But I don't scare easily.'

At the same time I heard a peculiar *whooshing* sound coming from downstairs. It was followed by a shrill, panic-stricken cry.

It was Hettie. She was in danger.

The Rascal's thirteen second warning seemed to have come true.

11.'MAY THE BEST SPY WIN.'

I left the dummy to do what he did best (very little, no offence intended) and hurried out of the Rascal's Bedroom.

Bad move.

Don't ask me how, but smoke had engulfed the entire tower. Wary of walking blindly into the unknown, I slowed to a pace even a snail would've been ashamed of and shuffled over to the stairs. Thankfully, I was still on my feet when I eventually found them. That, however, was soon about to change.

Fearing a tumble, I took a seat and began to slide down towards the first floor one step at a time. The lower I got, the thicker the smoke became, so much so that by the time I had reached the bottom I could no longer see my own fingertips (my hands, admittedly, were behind my back, but I won't tell if you don't).

'Hettie!' I called out. 'Where are you?'

I listened carefully, but there was no reply. Cautiously, I edged towards the two doors. Both of them were closed. If I was going to find Hettie then I would have to move fast.

Starting with the door on my left, I pressed down on the

handle and was about to charge inside when I felt a hand on my shoulder.

'Got a memory like a goldfish, have we?'

I turned sharply. I couldn't see much beyond the smoke, but I still recognised the voice. It was Hettie. 'What was the question again?' I mumbled. 'Oh, yes. Goldfish memory? Maybe. I can't remember.'

'Stays out or else!' Hettie popped up in front of me and pointed at the sign on the door. 'All come-coming back to you now, isn't it just?'

'Indeed it is,' I frowned. 'Still, at least I would've made it down to the ground floor that little bit quicker.'

'Quicker, yes ... but with two limping legs and a squashed skull,' remarked Hettie, a little too honestly for my liking. 'Easier-peasier just to use the stairs like a normal human body.'

'What were you saying about a memory like a goldfish?' I cried. 'You do know that Hag's Hole is on fire, don't you?'

'Nope,' replied Hettie. 'Don't know what's never been true.'

'It must be,' I insisted, peering around in desperation. 'You can't have smoke without fire.'

'Can,' replied Hettie stubbornly. 'Especially if some sneaky stinker has put smoke bombs through your letterbox.'

I screwed up my face. 'Smoke bombs?'

'Watched them with my own peepers,' Hettie revealed. 'One blinkety-blink later and smoke was anywhere and everywhere. Two blinkety-blinks and I spotty you, bouncing down the stairs on your bot-bot.'

'I wanted to check that you were okay,' I explained, placing a hand on her arm. 'I heard you cry out.'

'Heard that, too,' nodded Hettie, 'but me it most certainly was not. Must've been some other screamer.'

'Some other screamer … like the Rascal?' I said, raising an eyebrow.

'Possibly possible.' Hettie took a step to one side so she could look behind my back. 'Guessing you didn't catchy him then,' she sighed.

'You guess correctly,' I shrugged. 'But I will do. That's a promise. A pinky promise from Pinky Weasel.' I remembered the scroll I had found inside the dummy's mouth. The Rascal had told me where I would find him – Mysterious Melvin's Museum of Mind-Bending Marvels – but he wouldn't stay there forever. 'There's somewhere I need to be,' I announced. 'Somewhere that isn't Hag's Hole. You will be alright on your own, won't you?'

'Ha! What a chuckle that is!' laughed Hettie. 'Only been living here sixty odd years and six. Sure I'll be fine and dandy. As for you, Weaselly, take care and let care be taken. Dangerous is the Rascal. Very muchly so.'

'He's not the only one.' With that, I set off down the stairs towards the ground floor. The smoke may have cleared enough for me to see where I was going, but that still didn't stop me from staggering and stumbling several times before I reached the bottom step. Moving over to the door, I picked up the smoke bombs and shoved them down the front of my trousers for safe keeping. In hindsight, maybe I should've thrown them back through the letterbox. I could even have tried to unlock the door and leave the house that way as well. I, however, don't tend to think like a normal person and headed straight for the least obvious exit point imaginable.

The cat flap.

I spotted Pudding as I dropped down on to my hands and knees. I offered him a friendly smile, but then tried not to get offended when he didn't smile back. If it wasn't for that cat (or rather the old cat before he went on his crash diet) then I would never have got into Hag's Hole in the first place. And if I had never got in, I would never have found out that the rumours were true.

The Rascal was real.

The day had almost dawned by the time I had wriggled my way outside. It was light, just not as you'd know it. Certainly not bright and beautiful. That would've been a miracle for somewhere as dull and dreary as Crooked Elbow. No, this was more of a murky half-light. Bleak seemed to sum it up perfectly. Still, at least it wasn't raining.

Oh, why did I say that?

Scrambling to my feet, I pulled the smoke bombs out of my trousers and tossed them into the overgrown back garden as the first droplets of a rainstorm splattered against my forehead. I didn't wait for the bombs to fizzle out, choosing instead to race around the side of the house before swerving towards the gate. I sped up when I hit the pavement. There was still nobody in sight, which meant that there was still nobody to get in my way. I did a quick calculation and decided that if I continued at the speed I was currently travelling at I could make it to the museum in exactly eighteen minutes and forty-one seconds time. I had no idea if the Rascal would still be there by then, but there was nothing I could do about that. Try as I might, I couldn't go any faster. Not with the rain drenching my over-sized trousers and my clown-like loafers squelching beneath my feet.

No, whether I liked it or not (and I didn't), all I could do was cross my fingers and hope for the best …

Wrong.

As it turns out, I could go faster. A whole two seconds faster.

It took me eighteen minutes and thirty-nine seconds to get to Mysterious Melvin's Museum of Mind-Bending Marvels … and less than a split-second after that to realise it was lucky to still be standing. A mouldy-looking building that had been left to turn a grotty grey colour over time, I tried to ignore the fact it was both crumbling at the corners and eroding at the edges and concentrated, instead, on the entrance. A dozen or so decaying steps led up to a set of grimy glass revolving doors. I had almost reached the first of these when something made me stop. I could sense a presence. Almost as if I was being watched.

The most obvious place for anybody to hide was in the car park. Now, I'm no expert when it comes to cars, but, of the three that were in view, one was red, one was blue and the other was black. Parked in a row, not far from where I was stood, all of them appeared to be empty. I, however, knew better than to trust my eyes from such a distance and began to edge towards them.

'Watch where you're walking, Weasel!'

The voice stopped me mid-step. If I didn't know better, I would've said it was coming from somewhere near my feet. When I *did* know better, I almost fell over from the shock of what I saw.

To my horror there was a head in the road.

Yes, a head.

Just a head.

'How is that even possible?' I spluttered.

'How is *what* even possible?' Pushing herself up, Violet Crow – also known as Agent Sixteen – revealed the rest of her body as she climbed out of the manhole in the middle of the car park.

'Phew, that's a relief,' I sighed. 'For a minute there I thought you'd been … oh, it doesn't matter. What are you doing here?'

'What does it look like?' snapped Crow, her eyes darting from left to right as she placed the cover back over the manhole. 'I'm searching for the Rascal.'

'Down there?' I laughed. 'In the sewers? That's a bit extreme, don't you think?'

'Not at all,' scowled Crow. 'The Rascal could be anywhere … and I'm prepared to go to any lengths to prove it.'

'Maybe so, but you're still looking in the wrong place,' I insisted. 'The Rascal is in the museum. He told me so himself. You're free to tag along if you—'

'Tag along?' Crow shook her spiky head in disbelief. 'I'd rather stick both my elbows together with super glue than team up with you. I said at Hag's Hole that I'd catch the Rascal first … and that hasn't changed! You go your way, Weasel, and I'll go mine. May the best spy win.'

'I will.' I was about to wink at Violet Crow when, without warning, she raced across the car park and dived over the first of the three cars. She disappeared from view before I could ask her if it hurt. Not to worry. I had wasted enough time already arguing with the angriest spy in Crooked Elbow.

Now it was time to beat her to the prize and shut her up for good.

I skipped up the museum steps before they fell away beneath my feet and then stopped at the revolving doors. The glass was covered in a combination of chips and cracks, not to mention numerous smeared fingerprints, but none of it was enough to stop me from noticing the paper scroll that had been pushed between the grooves.

I snatched it without thinking and then read it whilst I caught my breath.

> *To the spy who seeks me,*
>
> *If we're going to meet, then you'd better come on in. Don't try too hard to find me, though, because there's really no need.*
>
> *Be seeing you, the Rascal.*

I was about to read the scroll again when, as if by magic, the glass revolving doors began to do just that. They were revolving. The Rascal had told me not to try too hard and this was why. By the look of things, all I had to do was wander in, keep my eyes peeled and the Rascal would appear before me. It was that simple.

Wasn't it?

With my walking stick in one hand (and my other hand holding up my over-sized trousers), I passed through the doors and entered Mysterious Melvin's Museum of Mind-Bending Marvels for only the second time in my life …

… and then instantly regretted it.

12. 'WE HAVE YOU SURROUNDED!'

Like its name suggested, Mysterious Melvin's Museum of Mind-Bending Marvels was packed from floor to ceiling with ... *erm* ... mind-bending marvels.

I'm guessing you figured that out for yourself, but, just in case you didn't, let me throw out a few examples to help you understand just how mind-bending things really were. Have you ever seen a television made of jelly? No, thought not. Or an inflatable werewolf? Bit weird. Or what about a walking, talking lamppost? Dressed in a space suit? With teeth? Yes, that's a *lot* weird. And completely pointless, of course.

That was nothing, however, compared to the security guard that was sprawled out across the floor in front of me.

Laid flat on his back with his eyes tightly shut and his mouth wide open, it was the peaked cap and green uniform that gave him away. Oh, and the badge that was pinned to his chest with *Security Guard* printed on the front. Just below it, *Garth* had been written in thick blue pen. For a moment I wondered if he was part of the museum, before quickly deciding that even Mysterious Melvin would find it too mind-bending to put such an unusual thing on display.

No, as far as I could tell, Security Garth was one of three things.

Asleep, unconscious, or dead?

I knelt down by his side, rolled up his trouser leg and tickled his bare ankle. He didn't wake up which meant that he couldn't be asleep. Not only that, but now I was much closer I could see that his chest was gently rising. He was breathing. And dead security guards don't usually breathe.

That just left unconscious. Got there in the end, didn't we?

Call it a spy's sixth sense, but this was no accident. It was deliberate. Double deliberate with an added dollop of deliberateness. Someone had knocked poor Garth out on purpose. And it didn't take a genius to figure out who.

Before I could lay the blame at the Rascal's slippery feet, however, my attention was drawn to the museum's display. Or rather, what was missing. Security Garth was laid on the exact same spot where you would normally find a chocolate skateboard. I only knew this because of a small cardboard placard advertising the fact. The skateboard hadn't been squashed or squished, it didn't appear to have rolled away, and it was far too big to eat in one sitting. It left me with no other option but to assume the assumable.

The skateboard had been stolen.

I was still staring at the lifeless body by my feet when the same lifeless body did something quite unexpected and began to stir. One after the other, Security Garth's belly bulged, his bottom burped and two of his shirt buttons popped open. To my surprise, a paper scroll emerged from out of the gap. I carefully removed it, wiping it clean on my trousers before daring to read what had been written inside.

To the spy who seeks me,

Thank you for joining the party. Unfortunately, I've already left, but you weren't to know that. Move quickly, however, and you'll be able to catch the train to Twisted Kneecap. It departs the Crooked Railway Station at 9.34 in the morning. As for now, this is your thirteen second warning.

Use your time wisely, the Rascal.

My brain was turning cartwheels as I tucked the scroll back inside Security Garth's shirt.

Two things worried me in particular. There was no way the Rascal could've known when I would get to the museum or even if I would read his scroll, which meant he either had magical powers – unlikely – or he was watching my every move – more likely. Ever since I had first turned up at Hag's Hole, he was always one step ahead of me. But only one step also meant that he had to be close. Closer than close. Just not close enough that I could actually see him.

The other thing that worried me was the Crooked Railway Station and the nine thirty-four to Twisted Kneecap. They worried me because neither existed. Not anymore. Not since the station had been boarded up and the trains had stopped running. That was over two years ago now, when the Elbow Underground had opened and swiped all the commuters for themselves. Why did the Rascal think I could join him on a train when no such train even existed? Was this his first mistake? Or was it just me who was (once again) mistaken?

I heard sirens in the distance and remembered my thirteen second warning.

Springing into action, I hopped over Security Garth before skidding to a halt by the revolving doors. I was just in time to see four police cars pull up by the steps. A moment later and eight officers from the Crooked Constabulary had bundled out of three of the vehicles. Both fully clothed and fully armed, the officers looked more than able to catch a criminal. A thief perhaps.

A thief that had knocked out a security guard and then stolen a chocolate skateboard.

A thief that the police would wrongly assume was me.

The Rascal had done it again. He had trapped me and tricked me and played me for a fool. Unfortunately, I had played the part to perfection.

I dropped down, out of sight, as the last of the vehicles opened and a short, slight man appeared at the foot of the steps. Dressed in a long, beige trench coat, he had an immaculate side-parting in his hair and a fake moustache painted above his top lip. I knew this because we had met before.

His name was Detective Inspector Spite.

Except that couldn't be. It couldn't be because Spite was locked up in the Crooked Clink after helping to smuggle a bucketful of diamonds into the Pearly Gates Cemetery. Or so I thought. He wasn't, of course, because I could see him now, coming up the steps towards me, carrying a megaphone that, any second, he was about to speak into …

'We are the police! We have you surrounded! Give yourself up now!'

When Spite spoke, every word arrived with a short, sharp whistle as if his teeth didn't fit together properly. Under normal circumstances, I would've found that extremely amusing, but these circumstances were anything but normal. In a moment's time, Spite and his eight officers from the Crooked Constabulary would reach the glass revolving door and see me hiding in the museum.

There was no way I could let that happen. Not now, not ever. And that was why I had to make a break for it. Cut and run. Get out of there.

So, guess what?

That was exactly what I did.

13.'I'VE … I'VE FOUND A DEAD BODY!'

I turned my back on the advancing Detective Inspector Spite and the Crooked Constabulary and headed back into Mysterious Melvin's Museum of Mind-Bending Marvels.

Unfortunately, I forgot about what was sprawled out across the floor.

Security Garth was still yet to move when I tripped over his legs and took an almighty tumble. I hit the ground with a *thump*, but, unlike Garth himself, I couldn't stay down for long. Not with Spite right behind me. Yes, he was about to enter the museum any second now, but that didn't mean I had to be the first thing he saw when he did so.

Scrambling to my feet, I ignored the vast array of curious curiosities on either side of me and hurried towards a staircase I had spotted at the other end of the room. I got there in a matter of strides and began to head on up, careful not to trip over the Big Cheese's trousers in the process. By the fifth step, however, the revolving doors began to turn and the air was filled with the repetitive stomp of heavy boots.

I stopped suddenly and held my breath.

Too slow, Hugo.

'The thief may still be here,' bellowed Spite through the megaphone. 'Search every nook and cranny until you find him.'

I crouched down and tried desperately to hide behind my hands. I was in a sticky situation and there was no obvious way out of it. If I decided to run they would see me for sure and if I stayed where I was they would find me for certain.

Should I stay or should I go?

I was still struggling to make up my mind when I heard another voice ring out around the museum.

'I've ... I've found a dead body!'

I guessed it was one of the police officers. I also guessed that they hadn't found a dead body at all.

No, what they had found was Security Garth.

I peeked between my fingers to see what was going on. As far as I could tell, every one of the Crooked Constabulary had gathered around the security guard, whilst Spite had gone one step further and was now prodding him on the forehead with his megaphone.

No one, however, was looking in my direction. Not even close.

So, I asked myself the question again – should I stay or should I go?

Go.

Thankfully, the security guard still hadn't come around as I hopped, skipped and jumped my way to the top step. Which – don't take it personally, Garth – was perfect for me.

I took a breath or two as I shuffled away from the

staircase. In through the mouth and out through the nose. Definitely no snorting. What now? To my left there was a post box made of flowers, to my right there was a glass trampoline and straight in front of me, blocking my way, there was a bath tub filled with cold gravy.

Then I saw it. Stuck in the furthest corner of the room, partially obscured by the smallest caravan ever created, it was neither mind-bending nor a marvel. It was just a door. The fire exit to be precise.

Or, as I like to call it, my way out of there.

I crept over and gave the door a gentle push. I half-expected it to trigger some kind of alarm, but nothing happened so I pushed a little harder. Sure enough, the door moved to one side and I slipped through the opening.

Now I was outside.

On the roof.

The first thing I felt was a bitter blast of cold air. The rain may have come to an unusually early conclusion, but the wind was a perfectly able replacement. Shielding my eyes from the stormy gusts, I scampered over to the edge of the roof to see what I was faced with.

A long drop, that's what.

That's the problem with any roof. There's only one way to go … and that way is always down! I screwed up my face as I peered at the ground beneath me. I had been in this kind of situation before and jumped. Okay, so it hadn't been a particularly enjoyable experience – to be honest, it was one of the most terrifying moments of my life – but at least I had survived. Just.

That didn't mean, though, that I would survive for a second time …

My over-sized trousers started to billow in the breeze so I carefully stepped away from the edge for fear of getting blown off. As luck would have it, the wind chased me all the way back towards the fire exit before I did something I'd soon regret. Whether I liked it or not, the roof was a no go.

Heading back into the building, I listened out for any sound of Detective Inspector Spite and his megaphone, but there was nothing to hear. Maybe he had got bored of searching for me and gone off to bother somebody else.

Or maybe that was just wishful thinking on my part.

It was only when I reached the staircase that I heard the commotion coming from downstairs. Moving onto the top step for a better view, it didn't take me long to locate Spite and the rest of the Crooked Constabulary. They were just where I had left them.

Security Garth, however, was not.

Struggling to stand, he looked more than a little unsteady on his feet, but at least he seemed okay. Shocked, certainly. And pale. Yes, very pale. But no longer unconscious (which, when all's said and done, was probably good news for everybody, even me).

Unfortunately, Garth's recent reawakening only confirmed one thing that I had suspected all along. Apart from the roof, there was only one way to get out of the museum and that was through the revolving doors. And how could I do that without walking straight past Spite?

Answer … I couldn't.

It left me no other option but to try the *untryable.* (Note to self. That might not be an actual word. But if it isn't, it should be.)

If I was going to board the imaginary train to Twisted Kneecap then I would have to think so far outside the box that my brain would be on one side of Crooked Elbow and the box would be on the other. It was time to do something unexpected. Something out of the ordinary. Something so completely and utterly unexpectedly out of the ordinary that only one person would ever dream of doing it.

And that person was me.

With that in mind (and precious little else if I'm being honest), I lifted one of the Big Cheese's loafers and began to stamp my foot. It didn't take long for Spite to follow the noise and spot me at the top of the staircase.

'I heard you were looking for a thief,' I called out. 'Well, look no further. I'm here.'

Told you so.

I hope that was completely and utterly unexpectedly out of the ordinary enough for you.

14.'WHERE DID IT ALL GO WRONG?'

Detective Inspector Spite glared at me in disgust as he placed the megaphone to his lips.

'You!' he cried.

'Yes, me,' I nodded. 'The one and only Pink Weasel. It's a pleasure to meet you again, Spite. You and your ridiculous moustache both look in perfectly good health—'

'My moustache is none of your concern,' spat Spite. 'Weasel, you are under arrest. Come down now with your hands in the air. I need to check that you're not carrying a weapon.'

I raised my arms above my head and set off down the stairs.

'Stop!' ordered Spite. 'There seems to be something … I can't quite tell … what exactly is that poking out of your trousers?'

'Oh, that's just my walking stick,' I replied matter-of-factly. 'Although, that's not to say that it's a stick that can walk—'

'Why do you need a walking stick?' asked Spite suspiciously.

'I'm older than I look,' I remarked.

'Well, you look about twelve,' frowned Spite.

'Precisely,' I said, grinning. 'I'm actually thirteen.' Bounding off the bottom step, I quickly made my way towards Spite before I had chance to change my mind. 'The walking stick was a present from my father,' I revealed. 'Admittedly, it wasn't a present for me, but … oh, will you please get that megaphone out of my face? It's so close I could stick my head inside and wear it like a hat!'

'I don't do what you tell me,' argued Spite, refusing to move the funnel-shaped device away from his mouth. 'And I'm not bothered about your walking stick. If it's not a weapon you can keep it. What I am bothered about, though, is you and, perhaps more importantly, the fact that you're even here. You're nothing but a two-bit thief. A worthless weasel in both name and character. I knew that before the day we met and I still know it now. And there's only one place someone like you ends up.'

'Well, it's funny you should say that because there is somewhere I need to go,' I said eagerly. 'If you fancy giving me a lift there then that would be wonderful.'

I crossed my fingers and then crossed my legs for good measure. Spite, regrettably, didn't seem to get the hint. Although, oddly enough, he did seem to be getting more and more irate.

'You don't get to choose where we go either,' he said angrily. 'I choose. Always me. No one else. And the place I was talking about is the police station. Now, as for you …' Spite turned towards the security guard and urged him to come closer. 'Is this the boy who knocked you out and then stole the chocolate skateboard?'

A still-shaken Garth was about to speak when I beat him to it.

'If I've stolen the chocolate skateboard, then where is it?' I asked. 'I've not hidden it in my waistcoat, have I? And I doubt anybody could eat that much chocolate in such a short space of time—'

'Do us all a favour and put a sock in it, Weasel!' shouted Spite. 'Or maybe even that walking stick if you're feeling really generous!'

'The thing is,' began Garth, rubbing his eyes, 'the boy has got a point.'

'No, he hasn't,' argued Spite. 'Just give me the facts and nothing else. Tell me that Weasel broke into the museum, hit you on the head and then stole the skateboard.'

'But what if he didn't?' wondered Garth.

'Well, he did,' insisted Spite. 'He must have.'

'I'm not so sure,' Garth frowned.

Spite pulled the security guard towards him. 'Just tell me what I want to hear,' he muttered. 'That there could be a chance, however small, that it was Weasel. That's not so hard, is it? Just tell me. Tell me. Tell … me … now!'

'Well, when you put it like that,' mumbled Garth. 'I suppose … there's always a chance—'

Spite pressed a hand over the security guard's mouth before he could say another word. 'Bad luck, Weasel,' he said, smirking at me. 'You've just been identified by our one and only witness.'

I shrugged my shoulders. Time was ticking by at an alarming rate. The imaginary train to Twisted Kneecap was departing soon and, even if I didn't think it actually existed, I still had to get to the old railway station to stand any chance of catching it. If I travelled there by foot I would be too late. By car, however, was a different matter altogether. By car I could get there on time.

Which got me thinking …

'What are we waiting for?' I said, holding out my hands. 'If you think I'm the thief then so be it. Take me away. Lock me up … and, whilst we're at it, get a move on … stop dawdling … please.'

Spite could barely conceal his excitement as he grabbed me by the wrists and slapped on a set of handcuffs. 'I'm pleased you've seen sense, Weasel,' he said, grinning from ear to ear. His face changed when he turned to address his officers. 'I'll take this petty pilferer back to the police station,' he announced. 'You lot can all do something else. Something useful. Like catching criminals. Yes, that'll certainly make a pleasant change.'

It was eighteen minutes-past nine when I finally exited Mysterious Melvin's Museum of Mind-Bending Marvels. Despite the handcuffs, I tried to give Security Garth a friendly thumbs-up on my way out, but I don't think he noticed. Not to worry. We weren't that close anyway.

Once outside, Detective Inspector Spite dragged me down the steps and then pushed me towards the nearest police car. He yanked open the rear door and, placing a hand on my head, forced me inside. I was about to complain when he slammed the door shut in my face.

'Sit there and don't move,' instructed Spite, as he climbed into the driver's seat.

'Sit there, don't move … but carry on speaking.' I didn't wait for Spite to say *no*. 'The last I heard you were on your way to the Crooked Clink for a lengthy stretch behind bars,' I remarked. 'So, where did it all go wrong?'

'You mean, where did it all go right?' A beaming Spite glanced at me in his rear view mirror. 'To get out, first you have to be in,' he explained. 'And I was never in prison. Not even for one day. There wasn't enough evidence, I'm afraid. A lot of it went missing. Purely accidental, of course. What a shame!'

'Yeah, what a shame,' I muttered. Unlike Spite, however, I meant it. 'Still, the truth always comes out in the end,' I added.

'You think?' laughed Spite.

'I know,' I insisted.

'You know nothing,' Spite cried. He pressed down on the accelerator and the police car sped off. 'I can't quite put my finger on it,' he began slowly, 'but there's something about you I don't like, Weasel.'

'Oh, there are *lots* of somethings about you I don't like,' I replied. Fortunately, Spite was too busy concentrating on the road to pay me much attention. 'Don't get me wrong,' I continued. 'I'm really enjoying this quality time we're spending together – not to mention the free transport you're providing – but I have got a question. I don't suppose we pass another station on the way, do we? Well, one in particular. The old railway station.'

Spite took a moment before answering. 'You're very strange,' he said (although I'm not the one who had painted a fake moustache under my nose, so I'll let you decide which of us is stranger). 'But, yes, we do pass the old railway station,' he revealed. 'In about one minute's time. Why do you ask?'

'No reason,' I said hastily.

But that wasn't true.

If I was going to catch the train then one minute was all the time I had to get both my hands out of the handcuffs and then the rest of my body out of the car.

One minute starting from … now.

15.'STOP THAT WEASEL!'

A minute isn't a very long time.

About sixty seconds as it turns out. Yes, I know. I was shocked, too. Still, if that was all the time I had then I would have to act quickly if I was going to put my plan into action.

Oh, did I forget to say? Of course I had a plan. I've always got a plan. Even when there's nothing to plan for.

With my eyes trained on the back of the seat in front of me, I slowly slipped one of my handcuffed hands into the pocket of the Big Cheese's waistcoat. It didn't take me long to find what I was searching for.

It was a tub. No, not a tub of ice-cream. This was much smaller, far warmer and nowhere near as tasty as that.

This was a tub of moustache styling wax.

I carefully removed it from the pocket and tried to unscrew the lid. I had barely started when the police car hit a bump and the tub flew out of my hands. I held my breath as it landed by my feet. The noise was sure to alert Detective Inspector Spite, but he didn't turn around. Phew. That was close. With the seconds racing by, I reached down and picked up the tub, ready for another go.

I tried again and, this time, managed to unscrew the lid. The tub was full to the brim with a white gloopy substance that was perfect for what I had in mind. Using the fingers on my left hand, I scooped up a huge dollop of the slippery, slimy moustache wax and then twisted my wrists as I tried to rub it underneath the handcuffs. I did this several times before switching hands. As far as I could tell, my plan was working. The cuffs were beginning to loosen. They didn't feel so tight anymore.

Unlike the time. That was tighter than ever. And disappearing fast.

Resting the tub in my lap, I scooped up the biggest dollop yet. Before I knew it, the handcuffs were sliding about all over the place. This was it. It was going to work. All I had to do was stretch my fingers … squeeze my knuckles together … and—

'You've gone unusually quiet,' said Spite, out of the blue.

I jumped at the sound of his voice. At the same time, the handcuffs fell off my wrists and bounced against the back of Spite's seat.

'What was that?' he asked, glancing over his shoulder.

'What was what?' I said innocently.

'That noise,' explained Spite.

'Oh, that noise,' I said. 'That was … my teeth!'

'Your teeth?' repeated Spite.

'Yes, my teeth,' I insisted. 'I'm just nervous. And … um … cold. That's why I can't stop my teeth from chattering.'

Spite seemed to enjoy that. 'You should be nervous,' he laughed. 'Very nervous … oh, there's the old Crooked

Railway Station that you were talking about.'

I looked out of the window and spotted three large archways, all of which were either chained or boarded up. Satisfied that Spite wasn't watching me, I shuffled a little closer to the door. I had to be ready. I doubted the car would stop which meant I'd probably have to do something I'd rather not.

And that was jump out of a moving vehicle.

Resting my fingers on the door handle, I took a deep breath and got ready to do just that when the police car began to slow.

'Typical,' muttered Spite under his breath. 'Traffic lights.'

My heart began to beat that little bit faster as the police car trundled to a complete stop. To my delight, the lights were on red.

But they wouldn't stay that way for long.

'Hey!' yelled Spite, spinning around in his seat as I jabbed at my seatbelt, pulled open the door and rolled out onto the pavement. 'What just happened?'

'I did,' I shouted back at him. 'Thanks for the lift. I didn't steal the chocolate skateboard by the way. Nor did I break into the museum and hit Security Garth. I'm guessing you already know that, though, don't you?'

I left the door open just to be awkward before clambering over the car's bonnet and hurrying across the road. With the railway station right in front of me, I targeted the middle archway. Two metal gates had been chained together, but there was still a gap running down the centre where they hadn't been secured properly. I skidded to a halt beside them and tried to pull them apart. The gap widened so I turned to one side and pushed my head through first before sucking in my stomach. It was impossible to tell if that would be enough …

It wasn't.

The gap wasn't quite as wide as I had imagined. Unfortunately, something had got stuck. And that something was me.

'Stop that Weasel!'

I looked back and saw Detective Inspector Spite rushing towards the gates. To my surprise he had left the police car stranded in the middle of the road so he could chase after me.

'Stop that Weasel!'

Thankfully, there was no one close enough to do as he asked. Not that I actually needed stopping. I had done a pretty good job of that myself trying to squeeze through the gates.

Spite reached out, ready to grab me, when an almighty smash stopped him in his tracks. It was coming from behind us. In the road to be precise. Exactly where Spite had left his car.

'No, surely not.' Spite hesitated, which gave me just enough time to wriggle some more. I was almost through when he took one last look at me. 'This isn't over, Weasel,' he snarled. With that, he ran back towards the road.

And I finally slipped through the gates. Safely inside the station, I didn't dare turn back in case Spite changed his mind and tried to follow.

The first thing I saw as I passed under the archway was a platform on either side of the tracks and a bridge that linked them both together.

But no trains.

As I expected, the station was deserted. Just me and a big round clock on the wall. At least that was working. The time was nine thirty-three.

I had made it with one minute to spare.

I walked forward and looked along the platform. There was nothing to see so I crouched down and put my ear to the ground. I could hear a strange humming sound coming from the direction of the tracks. I listened carefully and it seemed to get louder. So loud, in fact, that anyone would think a train was coming.

The clock said nine thirty-four. The exact same time as the train to Twisted Kneecap.

Right on cue, I saw plumes of thick, black smoke billowing into the air. And then, just a moment later, it emerged through the smoke.

It being a train.

I stepped back as it passed under the bridge and entered the station. An old-fashioned steam train with three carriages, it ground to a halt not far from where I was stood. With no time to waste, I raced forward, pulled open the door to the first carriage and climbed inside.

The train started to move as soon as I closed the door. I had made it. I was onboard the not-so-imaginary train to Twisted Kneecap.

And, fingers crossed, so, too, was the Rascal.

16.'I'VE JUST GOT ONE OF THOSE FACES.'

I held on to the hand rail as the train departed the old Crooked railway station.

There was no sign of the Rascal, but then there was no sign of anybody. There wasn't even a sign of any signs. No, as far as I could tell, the carriage was empty. Not a soul in sight.

But there was a scroll. It was resting on the first seat I looked at, waiting patiently for me to pick it up and read it.

To the spy who seeks me,

Oh, this is awkward. I hope you weren't actually expecting to find me in this carriage, because that's not what I said. There is a Rascal at Junkin' Jack's Scrap Shack, though, but you'll have to get off the train first. That won't be easy. Confused? You should be. Still, all will be revealed soon. About thirteen seconds to be precise. You must be familiar with my warnings by now.

Stay safe out there, the Rascal.

Feeling frustrated, I collapsed into one of the many free seats, scrunched the scroll into a ball and threw it over my shoulder. To my surprise, it rebounded off the headrest behind me, flew past my face and landed down by my feet. I tried to stamp on it, but missed completely and trod on my other foot instead. It should've hurt, but I didn't even notice. That's how angry I was. Angry that the Rascal was messing me about, pulling me this way and that to his heart's content. He was playing games with me … and I was stupid enough to play along with him.

I dropped to the floor, ready to retrieve the scroll so I could rip it into shreds, when I realised the thirteen seconds were up.

And that was the exact moment I heard a voice.

It was a man's voice and it was coming from one of the other two carriages.

Whether I liked it or not, I had company.

I stayed down whilst I considered my choices. My heart told me to follow the voice and find out who it belonged to, whilst my head preferred to hide out in the first carriage until the train came to a halt and I could get off.

Somewhat predictably, my heart trampled all over my head without even breaking sweat.

Okay, so the voice definitely didn't belong to the Rascal – he had already informed me that he wasn't onboard via the scroll – but it had to belong to someone. And that same someone might have an idea how I could get off the train (preferably when it wasn't on the move, of course) and then make my way to the curiously named Junkin' Jack's Scrap Shack.

Seeing as I was already on my hands and knees, I decided to stay that way and began to crawl along the carriage floor. The train shuddered from side to side as it sped along the tracks, but I refused to let it knock me off-balance. I stopped when I reached a glass door and took a sneaky peek into the next carriage. That, too, seemed to be empty, but I couldn't be sure. Wary of what might be lurking inside, I waited a few seconds to see if anybody stepped into view before opening the door and crawling through.

Not only was the voice even louder in the second carriage, but now I could make out some words as well. There was one that stood out in particular. Spat out with great gusto, it seemed to be repeated again and again.

Diamonds.

I ducked down behind the nearest seat I could find. I had come across a gang of diamond smugglers before, on my very first day as a fully-fledged spy. They were called the Majestic Mob. Both immaculately turned out yet incredibly volatile, they were one of Crooked Elbow's more sophisticated criminal families. The chances of it being them, however, were pretty slim. I'd say virtually impossible. No way whatsoever.

I slipped back into the aisle and set off, once again, on my hands and knees towards the third and final carriage. This time I moved at a much slower pace; careful not to make even the slightest of sounds. The closer I got to the glass door, the more I could hear. Oddly enough, the voice that I had heard originally was actually the quietest of all, albeit with an authority that would make most people stop what they were doing and pay attention.

Sure enough, that was exactly what I did when I waited at the door and let my ears do the hard work.

'There is no need to look so nervous, my fellow mobsters,' began the softly-spoken man. 'We are the most cunning, the most conniving, the most magnificent gang in the whole of Crooked Elbow. Smuggling is in our blood. Even now, it runs like a river through our victorious veins. What we are attempting today is both completely secret and absolutely fool proof. In all my years I have never met a rogue or wrong 'un who would dare to transport diamonds across the country using a decrepit old train on abandoned tracks. And yet that is exactly what we are doing now. Quite simply, we are unstoppable.'

Lifting my head, I peeked through the glass and took in as much as I could. There were one … two … three … four … five people inside the third carriage. Three women and two men. Dressed smartly, in either a long dress or a dark suit, they were all gathered around a circular table directly opposite me.

Then I saw him. The sixth person. Impossibly tall and impeccably dressed in a top hat and tails, he was pacing up and down the carriage with a cane in his hand and a scowl on his face.

His name was Marmaduke Archibald Pomegranate Majestic The Third.

Or Duke Majestic to those who knew him best.

Nickname Diamond Duke.

From a distance, he seemed like a perfectly respectable

member of society. Up close, however, he was anything but. His skin was pale, his eyes were black and there was a fierce scar running across the length of his neck. As the head of the Majestic Mob, it was he who pulled the strings, gave the orders and generally ran the whole show. Yes, we had crossed paths before, although when I say *crossed paths* what I really mean is he had pulled me out of an open grave at the Pearly Gates Cemetery and then told me to go away. Nothing to do with paths then. Although he had been really cross when he had done it.

I ducked down so I could gather my thoughts. I wasn't here for the Majestic Mob. If I got involved now I might regret it later on.

I actually regretted it much sooner than that.

About three seconds, in fact.

That was when two rough hands grabbed me under my armpits and lifted me off the ground.

'Don't try anything stupid,' snarled a gruff voice in my ear.

'I never try,' I replied. 'I just do it by accident. It comes naturally. It's a speciality of mine … whoa!'

The train jerked and I accidentally fell backwards into Rough Hands. I hit him harder than we both expected and he let go of me. I landed with a *bump*, but stayed on my feet. That was when I decided to elbow Rough Hands in the gut. I knew I had made good contact when he gasped in shock. His next move was to try and grab me around the neck, but he was far too slow. Before his hands had even left his side, I had dropped down and dived forward …

Straight through the door.

Straight into the third carriage.

Diamond Duke stopped pacing as I landed in a heap by his feet. 'My, my, what have we here?' he asked. 'Aren't you going to introduce us to your little friend, Onyx?'

Rough Hands – apparently known as Onyx – took a huge step into the carriage and hauled me to my feet. 'This ain't no friend, Boss,' he grunted. 'I found him snooping about outside.'

'You've been gone so long I thought you'd got yourself stuck in the lavvy,' chuckled a woman with a round face and red cheeks. 'Is that where you came across the boy? Was he hiding under the sink? Or just curled up in the u-bend?'

'I did my toilet business ages ago, Ruby,' snapped Onyx, clearly offended. 'No, I was on my way back when I saw him. He was flat out on his belly … spying on us.'

'Spying?' I blurted out. 'Why would you say that? I've never spied in my life. Definitely not. That's crazy. Absolutely bonkers …'

I could've gone on like that for ages, but Diamond Duke had other ideas. Swirling his cane, he pressed it under my chin, forcing both my mouth to shut and my teeth to snap together.

'If you weren't spying on us, foul boy, what were you doing?' he asked suspiciously.

'I was just … erm … watching,' I mumbled awkwardly. 'Watching in secret.' In hindsight, that probably sounded a lot like spying. I took a moment to think of something better to say. Then I took another moment because I'd actually spent the first moment wiping the sweat from my forehead. 'I'm here … I'm here … I'm here because I want to join the Majestic Mob,' I said eventually.

A blast of raucous laughter rang out around the carriage.

'You?' Diamond Duke arched an eyebrow. 'You want to join … us?'

'That's it exactly,' I nodded. 'And it's not funny either. I'm perfect for the Majestic Mob. I'm smartly dressed like you guys for a start.'

A disgusted-looking Diamond Duke gave me a quick once over. 'You do dress in a manner befitting our organisation,' he had to admit. 'Even if your clothes are a little on the large size.'

'I've lost weight, that's all,' I explained. 'A *lot* of weight. And I've shrunk. I blame the Crooked Elbow weather. It's not my fault I always get caught in the rain. Don't let that put you off, though, because I've got other qualities that I'm sure will come in useful. I'm quick and slick and nowhere near as thick as the rest of these dim-witted dullards I can see before me. Oh, did I just say that out loud?'

The fact that Onyx had picked me up by my ears seemed to suggest I had.

'Put him down, please,' ordered Duke. 'As tempting as it may be, I'd rather you didn't throw him off the train like an unwanted oyster. Not yet, anyway. Not until I've got to the bottom of things. There's something about our intriguing little intruder that concerns me greatly, and it's got nothing to do with his dramatic weight loss and inexplainable shrinkage.' Diamond Duke moved the cane from my chin to my nose. 'No, I've got a ghastly feeling that we've met before … and I didn't enjoy the experience!'

'We've never met,' I lied. 'Not before. Or after. And definitely not any time in between.'

'You remind me of someone.' The scar on Diamond Duke's neck began to throb as he studied me more closely. 'Someone who I wasn't overly fond of.'

'I've just got one of those faces,' I remarked. 'Unbelievably handsome springs to mind—'

'Not to my mind,' said Duke rudely. 'Most people would describe you as hideously grotesque, but I'd go one step further and say you're uglier than that. No, there's something else about you … I think we've done more than just meet … we've spoken … at the Pearly Gates Cemetery … stop doing that, Emerald!'

Diamond Duke spun around before he could grill me any further and confronted a small, squat woman who was pulling on his sleeve.

'This is important, Boss,' Emerald insisted.

'I'll be the judge of that,' argued Duke, before turning his back on her. 'Tell me your name, foul boy, before I run out of patience and throw you from the train myself,' he said coldly.

'My … name?' I mumbled. 'Wow, what an interesting question! Not one I was expecting either. Now, let me think. It's on the tip of my tongue … wait for it … any second now … or now … or maybe now …'

Diamond Duke increased the pressure on my nose. 'It's not difficult.'

I was about to answer when Emerald beat me to it. 'This is more important than you think, Boss,' she said nervously.

'What is your name?' asked Duke, all the while ignoring her.

'*Really* important,' stressed Emerald.

'What is your name?' repeated Duke. 'What is your name?'

Emerald pulled a little harder on his sleeve. 'Really, really important, Boss.'

'Just tell me,' cried Duke. 'What is your … oh, will you please stop doing that?' Turning sharply, Diamond Duke raised the cane towards his fellow mobster. 'This had better be as important as you claim because if it's not—'

'It is,' said Emerald, as she cowered beneath him. 'Can't you feel it?' she asked, resting a hand on the side of the carriage. 'The train. It isn't moving anymore. We've stopped!'

17. 'I'LL GIVE THEM … YOU!'

Emerald was right.

The train to Twisted Kneecap had come to a complete halt. And nobody else but her had realised.

'Onyx, take Opal and go and see what's going on,' ordered Diamond Duke, waving his cane at the two biggest mobsters at his disposal.

Onyx and Opal both did as they were told and hurried out of the third carriage. Everybody else, meanwhile, moved over to the window so they could take a look outside. Everybody except me. I had a better idea up my sleeve and it involved me creeping slowly in the opposite direction. I was heading closer to the carriage door. Closer to my way out of there. Closer to … freedom.

'Leaving so soon?' Turning suddenly, Diamond Duke jabbed the cane towards my face. 'This whole train-stopping incident hasn't got anything to do with you, has it?'

'Of course not,' I replied. Diamond Duke didn't seem to mind me creeping so I continued to do so. I realised why a moment later, however, when I crept straight into the returning Onyx.

'It's the police,' he said, panting hard as he shoved me to one side. 'They're everywhere. They've blocked the tracks and there's no way past. We're … stuck.'

Duke's top lip began to curl. 'How has this happened?' he growled. 'Nobody outside of the Majestic Mob knows that we're using this train to smuggle diamonds. I trust all of you with my life. *Almost* all of you.' That was aimed at me. Then something else was aimed at me as well. His cane. 'It's only natural that if I were to suspect anybody it would be you … you … you never did tell me your name, did you?'

'No, I didn't,' I replied hastily. 'But that can wait, can't it? For now, we'll concentrate on the police. I'll be honest with you; I think they're here for me. Don't ask me why, but they seem to be under the impression that I broke into Mysterious Melvin's Museum of Mind-Bending Marvels so I could steal a chocolate skateboard.'

'Why would they think that?' asked Duke.

'Because they found me in there,' I said sheepishly. 'I was going to make a run for it, but then decided that a lift in a police car was a far better option. They were even kind enough to drop me off at the old railway station. That's why I think they've put two and two together and come up with this train.'

Judging by the ugly scowl on Diamond Duke's face, I could only assume that he didn't believe me. That is, however, until he asked one simple question. 'So, where's this chocolate skateboard now?'

'Melted … probably,' I said with a shrug. 'But then it wasn't me who stole it, so how would I know? It was the

Rascal. I don't suppose you … oh, forget it. All you need to know is that I'm Spite's number one suspect and it won't be easy for any of us to change his—'

Duke raised his cane, stopping me mid-flow. 'Do you mean Detective Inspector Spite?'

'Regrettably so,' I nodded.

'I know Spite well,' remarked Duke. 'Too well, some might say.' I was already aware of that, of course, but I wasn't about to admit it. 'Perhaps there's no need for us to panic, after all,' Duke declared. 'I'm sure I can come to some kind of agreement with the good Inspector.'

'What kind of agreement?' I wondered.

'The kind that involves the police moving to one side and allowing my train to pass through unhindered,' revealed Duke.

'And why would they possibly do that?' I asked.

'Because I'll give them what they want,' smiled Duke. 'I'll give them … you!'

I screwed up my face. Of course he would. I should've guessed.

'I think it's time we went and introduced ourselves.' Marching across the carriage, Duke spun me around by my shoulders and pointed me towards the exit. 'And only one of us is coming back!' he added, prodding me in the back of my head with his cane.

Both Onyx and Opal moved out of the doorway so we could squeeze past. I tried to protest my innocence, but Diamond Duke refused to listen as he led me through the second carriage and into the first. It came as no surprise when we stopped at the door that I had originally entered through.

'After you,' said Duke, pushing down on the handle. He followed that up by pushing me in the back.

Stumbling forward, I was powerless to stop myself from falling out of the train. There was a slight drop before I landed feet-first beside the tracks. I was surrounded by long grass that reached all the way up to my neck. Beyond that, there was a dense wooded area. Perfect for getting lost in. I would have to remember that if I ever got the chance to escape (fingers crossed).

I guessed at the time – about ten in the morning. Maybe one minute past – and worked out that we had been on the train for almost half an hour. A journey that length would leave you halfway between Crooked Elbow and Twisted Kneecap. Or, in other words, we were slap-bang in the middle of nowhere.

'Don't try anything silly,' warned Duke, dropping down beside me. 'If you run, I will catch you. If you fight, I will defeat you. And if you—'

'Ask lots of stupid questions?' I said, butting in.

'Then I will silence you,' threatened Duke. 'Permanently.'

I mimed running a zip across my lips, which seemed to satisfy Diamond Duke enough for him to take his eyes off me. That was all the encouragement I needed to stride through the grass towards the front of the train to see what was going on. I had only taken a few steps, however, before I felt the cane on my shoulder.

'Get back here!' hissed a voice.

When I turned around, the only bit of Diamond Duke I could see was the top of his hat. I guessed he was crouching down in the long grass. Either that or he was sinking in quicksand.

'We don't want them to see us,' Duke whispered. 'Not until we know where Spite is.'

I reluctantly ducked down beside him, but not before I'd looked towards the front of the train. There were several police cars blocking the tracks and a dozen or so officers lined up behind them. Then I spotted Detective Inspector Spite. He was heading towards the first carriage with the megaphone pressed to his lips.

'We have you surrounded,' he called out. 'Give yourself up now or face the consequences.'

'You heard him,' I said. 'We'd better go and—'

'Get back here!' ordered Duke. 'You're not going anywhere. Not yet, anyway. I need to speak to Spite first before I hand you over. Problem is I need to speak to him in private.'

'Oh, do you want me to leave?' I said, ready to do just that.

'Get back here!' I was starting to think it was Diamond Duke's catchphrase he said it so often. 'I need to speak to Spite in private away from the other officers, not you,' he explained. 'There has to be a way to get him over here on his own.'

'Problem solved.' Springing to my feet, I began to hop up and down whilst waving my hands above my head. 'Hey,

Spite!' I shouted. 'I'm over here!'

'What are you doing?' asked a stunned Duke, tugging at my waistcoat.

'Oh, too rude?' I said. 'Okay … let me think … how about … good morning, Detective Inspector, what an absolute pleasure it is to make your acquaintance again.'

Diamond Duke switched from my waistcoat to my trousers, but only succeeded in pulling them all the way down to my ankles. I pulled them straight back up again, but not before Spite had spotted me stood there half naked in the grass. Lowering his megaphone, he waved his hands and urged the rest of the Crooked Constabulary to join him.

'No, not them,' I shouted. 'Just you. You won't regret it.'

Spite hesitated for a moment before ordering the police officers to back away. 'This better not be a trap,' he said warily.

'Not that I'm aware of,' I shrugged. 'But then this isn't my plan so I'm not really the person to ask.'

Diamond Duke seemed to take the hint and climbed to his feet. I, meanwhile, decided to do the exact opposite and sat down.

'Marmaduke Majestic,' said Spite slowly. I could no longer see him, but I could hear the shock in his voice.

'Detective Inspector Hector Spite,' replied Duke. 'I wondered when we might meet again. And now here we are …'

'Yes, here we are,' agreed Spite. 'There's a lot for us to talk about.'

'Yes, there is a lot for us to talk about,' nodded Duke.

'Well, get on with it then!' I moaned. 'This grass has already soaked through my … ouch!'

I felt a sudden stinging sensation across my cheek as Diamond Duke flicked out with his cane. At least I knew the rules now. They were allowed to talk, but I wasn't. Charming.

'I was almost arrested by the police at the Pearly Gates Cemetery because of you,' began Duke, pointing an accusing finger at Spite. 'That's the real police, though. You, however, are the other kind. The kind who like to involve themselves in the criminal activities of the Majestic Mob.'

'Keep your voice down,' urged Spite, glancing over his shoulder. 'That's not something I want the rest of the Crooked Constabulary to hear. Besides, I don't break the law anymore. Not for the past few weeks anyway. These days I prefer to uphold it.'

'I'll believe that when I see it,' snorted Duke.

'That might be sooner than you think,' replied Spite curtly. 'The best way to uphold the law is to arrest wrongdoers … and I'm looking at one right now!'

I wriggled about in the long grass and tried to get comfortable. By the sound of things this was going to take a long time.

'What are you doing on that train?' asked Spite. 'Don't tell me you're smuggling diamonds again?'

'Then I won't,' replied Duke stubbornly.

'So, you are,' grinned Spite.

'Not necessarily,' argued Duke. 'And, even if I was, I'm not sure I trust you enough to come to any kind of deal. We tried that once before, remember? And it all went horribly, horribly wrong … thanks to you!'

Yes, this was going to take a really long time. So long, in fact, that I could probably nip off for a bit and then come back later when they had finished squabbling.

Or maybe not come back at all.

'You betrayed me,' spat Duke. 'You stabbed me in the back.'

'Well, you stabbed me in the back … and the front,' said Spite smugly.

'Well, you stabbed me in the back, the front and from top to bottom,' shot back Duke.

Slowly, careful not to make even the slightest of *rustles*, I began to shuffle backwards through the grass.

'That wasn't my fault,' insisted Spite. 'Things were going well. Both of us were on track to make lots of money. That is, until that pesky Weasel showed up and ruined everything.'

I was still shuffling when I realised they were talking about me.

'What Weasel?' asked Duke, confused.

'The only Weasel,' explained Spite. 'Pink Weasel. What have you done with him? He's wanted for crimes against a museum and its staff. And he stole a skateboard made of—'

'Chocolate,' growled Duke. He took a moment to compose himself before he spoke again. 'Are you talking about the boy on my train?'

'Of course I'm talking about the boy on your train,' frowned Spite. 'The same boy who called me over. This isn't the first time you've crossed his path though, Duke. You met him not long ago at the Pearly Gates Cemetery.'

I stopped shuffling and kept completely still.

'Of course … I knew I recognised him.' A furious Diamond Duke looked over his shoulder. 'He was here … beside me … where has he gone?'

'You've lost him, haven't you?' sighed Spite.

'No!' Diamond Duke swung back and forth with his cane, slashing at the long grass. 'He's not lost. I've just mislaid him … but not for long!'

18.'DID YOU MISS ME?'

'Diamond' Duke Majestic was right.

Almost.

He had mislaid me. That much was true.

He just hadn't mislaid me very far.

To be honest, I was less than a stone's throw away. Well within tossing distance. If he had bothered to look a little harder, in fact (both eyes without blinking), he would no doubt have spotted me. Fortunately, he didn't. And he was far too flustered to start doing it now.

'So, I was correct first time,' muttered Detective Inspector Spite, rolling his eyes as he edged towards the head of the Majestic Mob. 'You have lost Pink Weasel.'

'Don't say that!' snapped Duke, slashing at the grass with even more ferocity.

'I already have,' smirked Spite. 'And I'll say it again if you're not careful. Now, tell me the truth. What are you doing here with Pink Weasel?'

'I'm not *doing* anything here with Pink Weasel,' replied Duke, as he widened his search for yours truly. 'He just appeared on the train and told me he wanted to join the

Majestic Mob. We didn't take him seriously, of course. We just laughed.'

'Well, you're not laughing now,' grinned Spite.

The conversation seemed to grind to an abrupt halt. I wanted to sit up to see what was going on, but resisted the urge. Thankfully, the silence didn't last for long.

'It seems we find ourselves at something of a standstill,' remarked Spite. 'I want Pink Weasel, you want Pink Weasel and yet neither of us knows where he is.' Spite paused for effect. 'I suppose the next best thing would be for me to find the Majestic Mob with a carriage full of smuggled diamonds on a stolen train bound for Twisted Kneecap,' he said thoughtfully. 'Come to think of it, that's a whole lot better than Pink Weasel and a chocolate skateboard.'

'You wouldn't dare,' said Duke unconvincingly.

'Wouldn't I?' Detective Inspector Spite must have removed the megaphone from somewhere inside his coat because the next words I heard were blasted out loud. 'Crooked Constabulary, go … go … go!'

The urge was finally too great to resist and I peeked over the grass to see what was going on.

A lot as it turns out.

With Spite leading the way, the police had sprung into action and were now racing towards the train. My eyes darted from left to right, but one person was notable by his absence.

Diamond Duke.

Before I could ask myself where he had sneaked off to, he raced into view. At a guess, he had abandoned the other mobsters and was now trying to escape by heading deeper into the grass. Unbeknown to him, however, he was veering dangerously close to where I was hiding. So close, in fact, that if he wasn't careful he might just …

'Whoa!'

Travelling at speed, Duke failed to heed my warning and tripped over my legs. He tumbled over and hit the ground hard. Just not hard enough, unfortunately.

'You!' Duke pushed himself up before switching his attention to me. 'You're Pink Weasel.'

'The one and only,' I said, inching away from him. 'Did you miss me?'

I rolled over as the cane swished through the air and struck the dirt beside me. Then I rolled back again as Diamond Duke swapped hands and swung for a second time.

'Yes, I did miss you,' he said, grinning manically. 'Twice, in fact. But I won't miss again.'

Looming over me like a turbulent telegraph pole, Diamond Duke did have a point. Missing me again was practically impossible. Hitting me, though, was as easy as … I don't know … walking.

Which reminded me …

'You're about to feel the full force of my anger,' scowled Duke, pulling the cane back behind his head. 'And there's nothing you can do about it.'

'Isn't there?' I replied.

'No, there isn't,' insisted Duke. 'Obviously.'

'Not so obvious actually,' I argued. 'There *is* something

I can do about it. Let me show you …'

Reaching into my over-sized trousers, I removed the only thing I had at my disposal.

'That's … not what I was expecting,' said Duke, trying not to smile as I waved the walking stick from side to side. 'What are you going to do with it?'

'This!'

Without warning, I flicked my wrist and the stick extended. And extended. And extended. Duke stepped back in horror, but didn't step back far enough as it kept on coming and hit him under the chin. The shock of it was enough to make him lose his balance and stumble back into the long grass.

That wasn't the only thing he stumbled into, however.

'Remove your hands from my person,' cried Duke, struggling to free himself from the clutches of two police officers who had crept up on him unnoticed. If they had crept a little further they would've seen me, but then why would they? They had already caught their man. They weren't looking for anybody else.

I waited until a furious Diamond Duke was out of earshot before climbing to my feet. As luck would have it, I was just in time to see him being bundled into the back of a police car, whilst the other members of the Majestic Mob were rounded up and led away from the train. And that was that. As far as I was aware, everybody had been accounted for.

Everybody except me.

I was about to sneak off in the opposite direction when

something dropped down from the tree beside me.

'You're a very lucky Weasel.'

I moved, but not through choice. If I'm being honest, it was more of a jump. Both out of the grass and out of my skin. When I finally landed, I was surprised to find it was Agent Sixteen who had appeared at my shoulder.

'And you're a very lucky Crow,' I said, breathing a sigh of relief. 'Not many agents have the pleasure of working with me. You should feel honoured.'

'Irritated … not honoured,' grumbled Crow. 'And I'm not working with you either. I'm saving your sorry butt … as usual. Now why don't you shift that same butt before the police see you.'

Grabbing me by the scruff of my shirt, Violet Crow dragged me deeper and deeper into the grass. Before I knew it, we had passed into the wooded area I had spotted when Diamond Duke had first pushed me off the train.

'You're supposed to be searching for the Rascal,' remarked Crow scornfully. 'Not fooling about with diamond smugglers.'

'I was … I mean, I *am* searching for the Rascal,' I insisted. 'It's an ongoing operation. I've just … erm … wandered off course a little. Taken one wrong turn or twenty. Not to worry, though. I'll soon get back on the right track.' I took a moment to look around. 'One question, though,' I said, screwing up my face. 'Where are we?'

'They call it Back O'Beyond,' revealed Crow. 'Hardly anybody lives around here … for obvious reasons.'

I thought about the scroll I had found on the train and,

in particular, where the Rascal wanted me to head next.

'That's a shame,' I said. 'I was hoping to get to Junkin' Jack's Scrap Shack—'

Violet Crow spun around so suddenly that I stopped mid-sentence. 'Why would you want to go there?' she snapped.

For once, I considered my answer. And, for once, I decided to tell the truth.

'That's where I'll find the Rascal,' I said, confiding in her. 'He told me so himself so it must be true. We could always pair up if you—'

'Dream on,' snorted Crow. 'I'd rather pair up with a spy-eating squirrel. Besides, as I keep on saying, there's only one person who's sure to catch the Rascal … and we both know that person isn't you, Weasel!' Crow ran a gloved hand over her spiky head as we passed through the last of the trees and found ourselves, instead, at the foot of a rather large slope. 'I can take you to the Scrap Shack if that's what you really want,' she said eventually. 'It's at the top of Swill Hill. I have to warn you though. Junkin' Jack Trash is the most savage scrap collector that's ever been born. He's more beastly than a boil on the bum. More disgusting than dog food on your dinner plate. To be brutally honest, heading up there could be the worst mistake you've ever made. The worst *and* the last.' Violet Crow gave me a moment, probably so I could let her words sink in. 'It's your choice, I suppose,' she shrugged. 'Do you want to go to the Scrap Shack … or would you rather live a little longer?'

19. 'THIS AIN'T NO PLACE FOR A SQUIRT LIKE YOU.'

Of course I wanted to go to the Scrap Shack.

Why wouldn't I?

Yes, it was dangerous, but then everything was dangerous in the life of a spy. Sometimes I can't even trim my own toenails without getting one stuck up my nose. That's why I don't bother. I just leave them to grow really, really long. If nothing else, they're like a secret weapon that nobody's aware of. Perfect for stabbing rogues and wrong 'uns in the ankles when they're least expecting it.

This, however, was nothing like trimming toenails. This was something I *had* to do.

Whatever it took, whether I liked it or not, I had to find the Rascal.

As was the norm in both Crooked Elbow and Twisted Kneecap (not to mention Back O'Beyond by the look of things), it was still raining cats and dogs (other household pets are available) by the time Violet Crow had led me halfway up Swill Hill in search of Junkin' Jack's Scrap Shack.

This damp and dismal day, though, had thrown up one unavoidable extra.

And that was the unforgiving stench of rotten eggs.

'Is that you?' I asked, squeezing my nostrils together to block out the smell.

'Not funny,' scowled Crow. 'May I offer you a simple piece of advice, Weasel? Keep your mouth shut and your bad jokes to yourself. The last thing you want to do is alert Junkin' Jack to your arrival.'

Without another word, Agent Sixteen dropped down on to her stomach and slithered towards a fallen tree trunk not far from where we were. I watched her in awe before deciding that she probably expected me to follow in much the same way.

I didn't, of course.

'When would you like me to start keeping my mouth shut?' I asked, wandering casually up behind her.

'About five hours ago,' muttered Crow. 'When we first met. Now, get down so you can't be seen. Only a complete pigeon brain would fail to hide in such a scary situation.'

'Better fetch the bird seed then,' I said smartly.

'Not funny … again,' frowned Crow. She waited a moment before peering over the top of the trunk. I followed her gaze and spotted a tall steel fence a little further up the hill. There was a gate in the centre, plastered with numerous warning signs, all of which seemed to say the exact same thing but in a slightly different way.

Danger! No Entry! Go Away! Not Welcome!

Charming. It's a good job I'm not easily offended.

'That's Junkin' Jack's Scrap Shack,' remarked Crow, gesturing beyond the gates. 'As far as I'm aware it's just a dumping ground for rubbish. Even from here I can see at least six fridges and a dozen or so smashed-up cars—'

'Not to mention the odd motorbike or nine and more bent and busted tables than you could fit in your average classroom,' I added. 'There's no sign of the Rascal, though. Or anybody come to that. Although there is an old caravan at the very top of the hill.'

'That's where Junkin' Jack lives,' revealed Crow.

'And where the Rascal might be hiding out.' With that in mind, I snatched a quick breath and then stepped out from behind the tree trunk. 'I guess there's only one way to find out for sure,' I remarked.

'What are you doing?' hissed Crow, as I continued up Swill Hill. 'I did tell you how unpleasant Junkin' Jack is, didn't I, Weasel?'

'Yes, only about three thousand times,' I shouted back at her. I tried to ignore the rest of Crow's unhelpful comments before I finally found myself at the gate in the centre of the fence. It rattled when I gave it a good shake, but nothing more. Then I spotted the padlock.

'Not as easy as you thought, is it?'

For the umpteenth time that day, Crow had crept up on me unnoticed. She was good at that. Not that I'd ever tell her.

'No, not easy … but that doesn't mean it's impossible,' I argued. 'I just need to be clever. Well, cleverer than usual.

Hmm … let me see … I don't suppose you've got a hot air balloon in your pocket, have you? Or how about a spade so I can dig a tunnel? No? Never mind. The thing is … that does leave me somewhat stumped … what are you doing with that catapult?'

The fact that Violet Crow had produced such a weapon from somewhere about her person was odd enough in itself. Stranger still, however, was why she had chosen to kneel down beside me and run her gloved hand over the grass.

'You want to get into the Scrap Shack, don't you?' Crow picked up a stone and weighed it in her palm. 'Well, this is the easiest way to do it,' she said, slotting the stone into the catapult's sling.

'Is it?' I screwed up my face. 'Because I can't see anything in there worth firing at. Only that caravan.' Oh, surely not. 'Don't tell me you're going to fire at that caravan?' I said nervously.

'Okay, I won't.' Lifting the catapult to her eye, Crow carefully pulled back the sling … took aim … and let go.

I tried to follow the flight of the stone as it flew through a gap in the fence, but lost it almost immediately. The sound of breaking glass a moment later, however, was enough to convince me that Crow had hit her target.

'I think you smashed something,' I said, fearing the worst. 'You told me you weren't going to fire at that caravan.'

Crow shook her spiky head. 'No, *you* told me not to tell you that I was going to fire at that caravan,' she pointed out. 'So I didn't. But guess what? I did. I hope that makes sense.

Now, don't blame me if you never get out of the Scrap Shack alive. See you soon, Weasel … perhaps.'

With that, Violet Crow turned away from the gates and hurried down Swill Hill. Before long she was weaving between the trees of Back O'Beyond. And then … she wasn't. She had gone. Left me to it.

It being the moment the door to the caravan burst open and out stepped a tall, gangly man with flat hair, a wonky nose and patchy stubble all over his cheeks. Dressed in a pair of grubby brown trousers and a stain-splattered string vest, he didn't seem particularly pleased to see me (don't worry, I'm used to that).

'Lovely morning,' I called out.

'Who says?' bellowed String Vest, his mouth barely opening as he spoke. 'Nothing lovely about that hole in my window. That hole makes me mad. Madder than mad. Mad … with you!'

'Why me?' I asked innocently.

'Because it was you what did it!' grunted String Vest.

'Technically, it wasn't, but I can see why you might think that,' I reluctantly admitted. 'Why don't we just brush this whole window-smashing incident under the carpet … or even under your caravan … and start again?'

'Never.' String Vest's shoulders drooped and his hips swayed from side to side as he wandered closer to the fence. 'You shouldn't be here,' he said gruffly. 'This ain't no place for a squirt like you.'

'I'm not just any old squirt,' I insisted.

'Nah, you're a skinny squirt,' remarked String Vest. 'A

skinny squirt who's about to feel pain like my window.'

'Oh, I get it,' I said, nodding to myself. 'Pain … window pane … very clever. Now, if you can just go and fetch Junkin' Jack then I'm sure we can—'

'We can't,' argued String Vest. 'And I can't fetch Junkin' Jack neither. Because that be me. Jack be my name and my other be Trash. Junkin' is for family and friends only … or just family … not many friends … or even any …'

'It's a pleasure to meet you Mr Trash,' I said politely. 'Although it's not you that I've actually come to see. I'm looking for the Rascal.'

'The Rascal?' Junkin' Jack stopped talking so he could hack up a lump of something black which he spat on the floor. 'Didn't think no one knew about my Rascal,' he mumbled.

'Don't panic; it's nothing serious,' I lied. 'I just want a little chat.'

'My Rascal won't talk to you,' cried Junkin' Jack. 'Won't talk to no one. Now gets gone before I gets you gone! Right?'

'Wrong.' I tried to stand my ground, but somehow managed to trip over my over-sized loafers, sending me stumbling backwards. 'I'm not going anywhere,' I said, once I'd fully regained my balance. 'I know you're angry about your window, Mr Trash—'

'Angry?' A red-faced Junkin' Jack was practically blowing steam out of his ears as he turned around and marched back up the hill. 'You think this is me angry?' he shouted over his shoulder. 'No, squirt, this is me jolly. Really happy-smiley. Let me show you angry, though. So you know for next time.'

'Don't think me ungrateful, but there won't be a next time,' I called out. 'If I'm being honest, I'd rather we weren't even having *this* time …'

Junkin' Jack, however, wasn't listening. Yanking open the door to the caravan, he stuck two fingers in his mouth and whistled. 'Come on out, my beauties,' he yelled. 'Today be your lucky day. I got you somethin' real tasty to nibble on.'

'Nibble on?' The words stuck in my throat as I caught sight of what emerged from the caravan.

It wasn't the Rascal.

No, it was much, much worse than that.

20. 'WHY DON'T YOU COME ON IN AND SAY HELLO?'

Junkin' Jack Trash had company.

There were six of them in total. Like a cross between a pig and a wolf (depending on how good your eyesight is), they were all large in size, brown in colour and covered in spiky bristles. Their narrow heads led to an unusually long snout, either side of which were a set of sharp tusks protruding from the corners of their mouths.

'They look … pleasant,' I said, screwing up my face. 'Are they the rest of your family?'

'That they are,' nodded Junkin' Jack. With his arms swinging in time with his footsteps, he lolloped back down Swill Hill with his new arrivals in tow. 'Wild boar.'

'Bit rude,' I frowned. 'I was only asking.'

'Not you – *them*,' explained Junkin' Jack, gesturing towards his motley collection of beasts. 'These be my Razorbacks. I breeds them myself. They be my own creation. A bit of this, a bit of that and a bit of the other. Bad news for you is that they're hungry. Just lookin' at you now is enough to make their bellies rumble.' Junkin' Jack stopped to hack up another lump of something black which he spat out the corner of his mouth. 'The choice is yours, squirt,' he said, shuffling over to the gate. 'You wanna' get to my Rascal, you gotta' get past my Razorbacks. Unless, of course, you're too chicken …'

'Chicken?' I tried to laugh, but it sounded more like a whimper. 'You don't scare me … much.'

'Pleased to hear it.' A toothless Junkin' Jack was grinning from ear to ear as he fiddled with the padlock. 'Why don't you come on in and say hello?'

The padlock fell to the ground and the gate swung open. Before I knew it, Junkin' Jack was heading back towards the caravan. By the time I *did*, he had disappeared inside. Gone, but not forgotten. The rancid stench he left in his wake was enough to see to that.

Any hopes that the Razorbacks would follow their master (or father, I'll let you decide) up Swill Hill were quickly dashed when Junkin' Jack slammed the door to the caravan shut behind him.

Now what?

This wasn't the time to stop and think. Instead, I rearranged my cravat, steadied my nerves and marched straight through the open gate into the Scrap Shack. Not so difficult, after all, was it? If only Violet Crow had been here to see me.

My next move, however, wasn't quite so simple. To my horror, all six of the Razorbacks shifted to one side until they had positioned themselves in a line, blocking my path to the caravan.

There was no way past.

Never one to be beaten, I turned left and tried a different route. Sucking in my breath, I squeezed between two wardrobes that had been pushed together so they could support the weight of a cracked sink and an old park bench. From the outside, the Scrap Shack appeared to be nothing more than a complete mess, a massive jumble of junk, but that wasn't really the case. The rubbish hadn't just been dumped and discarded like I had first imagined; no, it had been placed strategically to create a curious maze-like effect. If you veered off-course you could easily get lost in there. And if that happened, who would ever find you?

I put this to the back of my mind as I kept on moving up the hill. The junk was piled high on either side of me. So high, in fact, that there was no chance the Razorbacks could see me anymore. And if they couldn't see me, maybe they would forget about me. And if they forgot about me then maybe I could get to the caravan without them even realising. Then I could grab the Rascal … the Big Cheese would live happily ever after … and I could be home in time for breakfast. Okay, a late breakfast, but better late than never …

A strange snorting sound stopped me mid-drool.

I wanted to turn slowly, but did the exact opposite and almost fell over. There were three Razorbacks behind me. Separated from the pack, they must have followed the path I had taken and ended up here. Hot on my heels. Close enough for me to smell (and wish I couldn't).

With one eye trained on the beasts and the other on

where I was heading, I began to tip-toe nervously up the hill. Before I knew it, the tip-toe had developed into a full footstep. And it wasn't a nervous footstep either. No, whether I intended to or not, I was running.

As were the Razorbacks.

They were faster than me. Even I could see that and I was doing all I could to ignore them. Powering along, at the speed they were going, they would catch me in seconds. Four at a guess. Three … two … one …

I stopped suddenly and spun around, hoping the shock would send the Razorbacks running in the opposite direction. My heart leapt as it seemed to do the trick. And then sank as they steadied themselves and came again. Before I knew it, I was surrounded.

Think.

What I needed now was some kind of weapon … and I knew just where to find one!

I had almost removed the walking stick from my trousers when the first of the Razorbacks attacked. Baying for blood, it leapt forward, dangerously close to where I was stood. With no time to waste, I held the stick at arm's length and began to spin my entire body around in a wide arc. The Razorback yelped in fright as the stick *swooshed* through the air, missing its snout by a matter of inches.

It worked.

But for how long?

Pirouetting on the spot with a walking stick was just a temporary fix to a very serious problem. It wouldn't take the Razorbacks long to figure this out for themselves and, when they did, they would surely find a way around it. Especially if they worked together. Like a team. Then they would be unstoppable.

Quit giving them ideas, Hugo.

I stopped spinning so I could rethink my strategy.

At least, that was what I tried to do. Yes, my body had come to a halt, but it had forgotten to pass the message on to my head. All that twirling had left me dizzier than a raccoon on a roller-coaster. I could no longer see the Razorbacks, but then I couldn't see anything so that was hardly a surprise. Worse than that, I knew what was about to happen next, not that I could do anything to prevent it. My feet stumbled, my legs gave way and I crashed against a colossal collection of cardboard boxes that were piled up beside me. I hit them so hard they began to fall.

And so did I.

Wary of staying down for too long, I tried to stand, but found it almost impossible to do so. As far as I could tell, there was something trapping my foot. I guessed it was one of the boxes, but then changed my mind when I looked again.

It was a crate.

I gave it a push, but it was heavier than it looked. Determined to shift it, I pushed a little harder, but it still wouldn't budge.

In all the confusion, the Razorbacks began to creep towards me. Now I was an easy target, powerless to fight back if – or rather, when – they decided to make their move.

Panic-stricken, I grabbed hold of the crate with both

hands and, instead of pushing it away, attempted to tip it over instead. With a better view of its contents, I could see that the crate was packed full of small grey canisters, all of which had a brightly coloured label stuck to the side. My mouth fell open as I read the warning that was printed in large, red letters.

Toxic!
Do not shake, rattle or roll!
And definitely do not drop!

The crate had already tipped before I could do anything about it. I held my breath as the canisters bounced on the ground beside me. And then continued to bounce several more times because once just wasn't enough.

I waited … but nothing happened. Maybe they were harmless, after all. Panic over.

A second after that, however, I changed my mind …

21.'GO SNIFF HIM OUT FOR ME.'

Whatever was inside those canisters, it wasn't happy.

It wasn't even mildly annoyed.

No, it was just really, really angry.

One by one, the canisters began to shake and shudder before suddenly exploding. I stepped back in wonder as a strange yellowy, gas-like substance filled the air. At first, it seemed quite amazing. And then it didn't. If anything, it was awful. Absolutely appalling, in fact. And that was all because of the smell.

Whatever was coming out of those canisters reeked worse than seventeen rotten eggs wrapped in a dead kipper that had been rubbed all over a wet dog. I had smelled this smell before. On Swill Hill with Violet Crow. Up close to the source, however, it was something else entirely. And that something else was ridiculously revolting.

I swivelled on the spot, before realising that not even swivelling could help me escape the stink. By now, it had entered my mouth and invaded my nostrils, making it difficult for me to breathe. My first thought was to loosen the Big Cheese's cravat. Okay, so undressing in public probably wasn't my best course of action, but that wasn't really my intention. Instead, I pulled the cravat up past my chin until it covered my mouth and much of my nose. That was better. At least I could breathe now.

As luck would have it, I wasn't the only one affected by the stench. The Razorbacks had gone oddly quiet, but that's not to say that they had gone altogether. Wary of being pounced on at any moment, I put my head down and continued to shuffle up Swill Hill. I tried to go faster, but couldn't quite bring myself to do so for fear of …

'Ouch!'

This time I collided with a pile of old car tyres. Stacked high like a big, bald, rubber tower, they were totally avoidable if I was concentrating. Which I wasn't. How could I? Not with that sickening stink refusing to fade away.

I put two and two together and decided that the best way to escape the smell might be staring me straight in the face. Slowly, so as not to lose my footing, I started to climb up the tower. About nine tyres high, it was wobbly enough to make me nervous, but not wobbly enough to topple over. Or so I hoped.

With the stink nowhere near as horrible at the top, I lowered my cravat and snatched a breath or two as I cast an eye over the grounds of the Scrap Shack. I guessed that the caravan was somewhere up ahead, maybe slightly to my right, but that was all it was. A guess. And jumping down and charging blindly into the unknown because of a guess wasn't a risk I was prepared to take.

No, what I needed now was a better view … and the best

way to get that was to keep on climbing.

There was another tower of car tyres piled high beside me and, beyond that, a crane. No, not the long-legged, pointy-beaked bird, but a machine. Set on four wheels, it had a large, grabbing claw to pick up and transport the scrap. The claw had been left in a raised position. Higher than I was now. Perfect for what I had in mind.

I stepped carefully onto the next stack of tyres. My plan had three parts. First, jump up and grab the claw. Then cling on for dear life whilst I worked out a route to the caravan. And then swing back onto the tyres. At a push, I reckoned I could hang there for about sixty seconds if I was lucky. Maybe sixty-one if I got a good enough grip.

Now it was time to prove it.

With my eyes trained on the crane, I leapt into the air and reached out in desperation. I winced as my arms wrapped around the claw. The metal scraped against my hands, shredding the skin on my fingers. The pain was immediate and hard to ignore.

Dangling in mid-air, I peered out across the Scrap Shack. This time I spied the caravan. From down below it was impossible to see, concealed as it was behind a battered and beaten-up minibus, but up high I had a perfect view. Not only that, but I also knew how to find it when I got down from the crane.

Straight up the hill. Dodge the dodgy minibus. And there it was.

I repeated it over and over until the route was ingrained in my mind. I had no idea how much time had passed, but my grip on the claw was beginning to weaken. Swinging back and forth, I tried to gain enough leverage so I could jump back onto the tyres. I was about to let go when I sensed movement beneath me. Glancing down, I stopped swinging immediately.

It was Junkin' Jack.

If he looked up now it would all be over.

'Come, my beauties.' On his command, all six of the Razorbacks appeared from nowhere and crowded around their master. 'Where's the squirt?' he asked, patting each and every one of them. 'He's here somewhere. Go sniff him out for me. Sniff him out … and then it's snack time for everyone!'

With that, the Razorbacks flew into action, dispersing in different directions in search of yours truly. Junkin' Jack watched them go and then turned to leave himself. I waited until he was out of sight before I started to swing again. I was in agony, but that would be nothing compared to the pain of falling. However much it hurt, I had to find one more big swing to get me back onto the tower of tyres.

But one more big swing wasn't enough.

Even before I had let go of the claw, I knew I wasn't going to make it.

I was aiming for the top tyre, but fell short and slammed straight into the centre of the tower instead. I tried to grip on, but my fingers had barely brushed against the rubber before I bounced off.

By the time I realised I was falling I had already hit the ground.

Landing on my side, I felt a sharp, stabbing pain fly up and down my body. I took a breath or three and tried to figure out if anything was broken. As far as I could tell, it wasn't. And if nothing was broken, then I could move.

That went out the window, however, the moment I felt something rub against my leg.

It was something hairy.

Something hairy like a Razorback.

22.'YOU'VE GOT THIEF WRITTEN ALL OVER YOUR FINGERTIPS.'

The Razorback began to lick my loafers.

I resisted the urge to pull my feet away and chose, instead, to wait and see if the beast got bored and wandered off.

It didn't.

To my dismay, the licking actually increased as the Razorback made its way slowly up my body. Drifting over my trousers, it lingered on my waistcoat before finally stopping at my head. A moment later I felt something wet brush against my cheek.

The Razorback was licking my face.

And that, for me, was one lick too many.

Scurrying on all fours like a human crab, I scrambled backwards until I was out of reach of its huge, slobbering tongue.

'No more,' I muttered. 'Now, run along like a nice, little piggy before I get angry.'

It didn't. Run along, I mean. And I didn't get angry. But

I did get increasingly nervous. Especially when the Razorback lifted itself up to its fullest height and began to move towards me.

It was getting ready to attack.

I knew it. It knew it. And now you know it, too.

Simply knowing it was going to happen, however, wasn't enough … now I had to do something about it as well!

The Razorback was about to pounce when I threw myself to one side. I was aiming for the crane. Not the claw this time, but the wheels that it was resting on. I rolled over when I landed and then kept my body as flat as possible as I crawled underneath the vehicle. The Razorback quickly changed direction and tried to follow, but didn't get far. The crane was too low to the ground and the gap between the wheels was too small for a beast that size.

Lucky me.

I didn't hang around to gloat as I emerged out the other side. Jumping to my feet, the aches and pains I had suffered falling from the tyres were pushed to the back of my mind as I set off in the general direction of the caravan. Even if I couldn't see it, I knew where it was.

Unfortunately, I had company.

Two more Razorbacks had shown up out of the blue. My legs seemed to sense the danger before my brain and began to weave in and out of the scrap. As a last resort I veered towards the minibus I had spied from the crane. I knew I had to reach it before the Razorbacks reached me.

And I did.

Skidding to a halt, I yanked on the handle, desperate to

get inside. The door shook, but it refused to open. I kept on yanking, but it was no use. The Razorbacks were almost upon me when I gave up on the handle and dived behind a rusty, old washing machine that had been dumped close by. The first Razorback was going too fast to either notice or stop and collided with the minibus. It hit it so hard that the door folded in on itself and the windows smashed.

The second Razorback, though, wasn't so slow to react. It had almost certainly seen me move. It knew where I was hiding.

I tensed up, ready for impact. If the second Razorback was anything like the first it was sure to charge without thinking, destroying both the washing machine and me in the process. It had already started its run up when the door to the caravan flew open, causing the beast to change both its mind and direction as it went to meet its master.

'I know you're out there, squirt,' yelled Junkin' Jack. 'I can smell you.'

Whether I was stinky or not wasn't really the issue. No, Junkin' Jack had only said he could smell me – not see me. Which meant he had no idea how close I was to the caravan.

'Get after him, my beauties,' Junkin' Jack roared. 'And this time, I'm coming with you.'

I kept perfectly still as both Razorbacks shot past me, before Junkin' Jack followed soon after. I was sure he'd look back as he disappeared down Swill Hill, but he never did.

I had done it.

Somehow, against all the odds, I had made it to the caravan without getting nibbled, nipped or gnawed on.

Climbing cautiously to my feet, I took my time as I stepped out from behind the washing machine. Then I started to walk, slowly at first, just in case a Razorback happened to pop up in front of me. The fact I didn't breathe until I reached the caravan only seemed to make matters worse. Nerves had taken hold and, try as I might, I couldn't shake them off.

This was it. The moment I set eyes on the Rascal.

Or maybe not.

Like the minibus, I yanked on the handle, but the door to the caravan held firm. This time, however, I knew exactly what to do. Stepping back, I gritted my teeth and prepared myself for the pain that was sure to follow. Yes, it was going to hurt, although I doubted a few more bumps and bruises would make much difference to my already broken body.

Shoulders hunched, I took my lead from the Razorbacks and charged at the door. I was about to hit it at full pelt when it suddenly burst open. With nothing to block my path, I carried on moving, tripped over the doorstep and landed face-first on the crusty caravan carpet.

When I lifted my head I was amazed to discover that I was eye-to-eye with the answer to all my problems.

I had found Rascal.

Just not *the* Rascal.

The one I was staring at wasn't even a man. It was a piglet. A piglet with a name tag around its neck.

A name tag that said Rascal.

'This can't be happening,' I moaned. 'Don't tell me I've risked life and limb getting into this caravan for nothing.'

The piglet let out a tiny squeal. 'You've got nothing to fear,' I said. 'I'm not going to hurt you—'

'No, but I'm definitely goin' to hurt *you*!'

I could tell without looking that whoever was stood behind me wasn't Junkin' Jack. No, this voice belonged to someone much bigger, much stronger and much more likely to cause me some serious physical damage if I gave them the opportunity.

I shifted from my front to my back; just in time to see a woman squeeze out of the caravan's tiny bathroom. She was dressed in a long apron that was splattered with dark red stains, and wellington boots that were caked in mud. Her hair was tightly curled, her ears were crumpled and her nose was squashed as if it had been flattened with a rolling pin. Her knuckles on both hands were marked with tattoos. Her left spelt out *HATE*, whilst her right read *YOU*.

I started to mumble. 'Sorry … I thought … no, I didn't … my mistake … who are you?'

'Who am I?' The woman rushed forward and stood on my chest, pinning me to the carpet. 'The name's Jackie,' she said. 'Jackie Trash. I'm Junkin' Jack's mammy.'

'Poor Jack,' I muttered.

Jackie Trash pressed down even harder and I struggled to breathe. 'Poor you,' she growled. Clicking her fingers, the piglet ran over to her. 'You were going to steal my Rascal. But she don't belong to you.'

'I wasn't … going to … steal her,' I panted. 'I thought … she was … a man.'

'A man?' Jackie leant forward, placing even more weight

on my chest. 'I don't believe you,' she said fiercely. 'I don't know much about much, squirt, but I do know a liar when I see one. And I'm seein' one now! You've got thief written all over your fingertips.'

'Let me … explain,' I gasped. 'Yes, I was going to take your piglet … but I'm not any more. I promise. Now, if you'll be so kind and remove your foot … I'll be on my way and we can forget about—'

'Oh, we can forget alright … forget about you leavin'!' A furious Jackie stepped to one side and hauled me up by my waistcoat. 'Thieves like you need to be punished,' she yelled in my face. 'And I know just the way to do it!'

23.'IT'S MAGIC TIME!'

I slowly opened my eyes.

Then I shut them again. It felt better that way. When they were open my head began to spin and the pain was unbearable if I tried to focus. It hurt so much, in fact, that anyone would think I had been hung upside down and then left to dangle like an odd sock on a washing line.

Oh, did I forget to say?

That was what had happened. Exactly that. Nothing more, nothing less.

From the end of the last chapter to the start of this one, Jackie Trash had used a length of rope to secure me to the ceiling of the caravan by my ankles. And that's where you find me now. No wonder my head was spinning.

I tried to put the pain somewhere I could forget about it whilst I forced my eyes to stay open. Even upside down I could still make out both members of the Trash family hunched over a small side table at the other end of the caravan.

'He's watchin' us, Mammy,' Junkin' Jack sniggered. 'That's good. I like it better when they're awake. I like to hear 'em scream.'

'You and me both,' grinned Jackie, planting a sloppy kiss on her son's forehead.

'Leave me like this for too long and I'll be doing more than screaming,' I muttered. 'I'll be heaving and hurling. Puking my guts up. Basically, the entire contents of my stomach will end up all over your carpet. Not that you'd notice …'

'Pukin's the least of your worries, squirt,' remarked Jackie. 'You should be more concerned about what we've got in store for you.'

'Oh, I'm not one to get my knickers in a knot,' I said, trying to keep my cool. 'I've been in worse scrapes than this. And I always seem to get out of them alive.'

'Not this time.' Junkin' Jack turned around and revealed an enormous knife with a large, rectangular blade. 'This is my bone chopper,' he said proudly. 'I always like to start with the fingers. Then the toes. And then any other bits that stick out. Make a lovely treat for my Razorbacks, they will. And Rascal. She's waitin' outside with the others.' Junkin' Jack stopped talking so he could hack up something black which he spat over his shoulder. 'Although I'll tell you now,' he said, 'all those fingers and toes I've been talkin' about, squirt … they belong to you!'

'Yeah, I figured that out for myself,' I sighed. 'Listen, Trash, you're making a terrible mistake. Do you know who I am? My name is Hugo Dare. I'm a spy. I work for SICK.' I hesitated. 'You have heard of SICK, haven't you?'

'Yep,' nodded Junkin' Jack. 'You were about to be sick in our caravan.'

'Not that kind of … oh, it doesn't matter,' I said quickly. 'What about the Big Cheese?'

'I've heard of cheese,' said Jackie. 'I like to put it in my bed. And my shoes. Sometimes I even eat it.'

I screwed up my face. Jackie was even weirder than she looked. They both were. If I was going to persuade either Trash to get me down then I would have to try a different approach.

'What are you scared of?' I asked.

'Scared of?' Looking more than a little confused, Junkin' Jack stuck his tongue between his last few remaining teeth and tried to think. 'Nothin',' he replied eventually.

'Well, that ain't true,' argued Jackie. 'You don't like toothpaste.'

'But I ain't scared of it, Mammy,' Junkin' Jack stressed.

'Fair enough,' shrugged Jackie. 'It's shampoo I don't like. It tastes funny.'

I was about to roll my eyes in despair, but then decided against it on the off chance they dropped out of their sockets whilst I was hung upside down. Toothpaste and shampoo were no good. If they had said snakes or spiders like most ordinary people I could have pretended I had seen one, or even that I had one hidden inside my waistcoat. If nothing else, it would've bought me a bit of time. As it was, I had nothing to go on.

'Magic,' remarked Jackie to my surprise. 'I don't like magic. And neither does little Jack. It puts the shivers right up our spines. The trembles in our toenails. The shudders in our shoulders.'

'Magic?' I cried out. 'You don't like magic? That's brilliant … no, not brilliant. Terrible. Yes, that's right. Absolutely terrible. For you two, anyway. And do you know why? Because that's what I am. Magic, I mean. I'm … um … a magician. I can do tricks. Lots of tricks. Things that are impossible to explain. So don't bother asking me what they are.'

Jackie let this stew inside her stodgy brain for a moment before poking her son.

'We don't believe you,' said Junkin' Jack unconvincingly. 'No squirt can do magic.'

'This squirt can,' I insisted. 'And I'll prove it if you're not careful. Come anywhere near me with that bone chopper and I'll have to get all magical.'

'You don't scare me,' barked Jackie. 'And don't let him scare you either,' she said, pushing her son towards me. 'Let's get chopping!'

I watched in horror as Junkin' Jack lifted my left hand and began to study my fingers. 'So many to choose from,' he mumbled to himself.

'That's it,' I cried. 'I warned you what would happen, but you didn't listen. It's magic time!'

Junkin' Jack rested the bone chopper against my little finger. 'I don't see no magic,' he smirked.

'Give me a chance,' I snapped back at him. 'I'm just warming up.'

'Chop it off … chop it off,' sang Jackie, from somewhere under her son's armpit.

'Don't listen to her!' I shouted. 'You'll regret it! You both will!'

Junkin' Jack's mouth fell open as he concentrated on the job in hand. I began to wriggle furiously as he raised the knife. The magic hadn't worked – largely because I didn't know any – so what now? If I wasn't careful Junkin' Jack would slice off my finger. And then another straight after. And another after that. And … do I really have to go on? Because I don't want to. I'd rather not think about it at all if I'm being honest.

Do something, Hugo.

I was still struggling to decide what that something could be when something did happen … and it had nothing to do with me!

For no apparent reason, Junkin' Jack dropped the bone chopper as he staggered backwards across the length of the caravan. He bumped into Jackie before she had a chance to move to one side; the force enough to send the two of them tumbling to the ground in a great Trash heap.

Whether I liked it or not, I, too, was on the move. Swinging back and forth, I couldn't stop my body from banging repeatedly into the side of the caravan.

What was happening?

Was it me?

Was it … magic?

Don't be daft. This was far easier to explain than magic. This was gravity.

Quite simply, when I had first arrived at the Scrap Shack, Junkin' Jack Trash's caravan was at the top of Swill Hill. Now, however, it wasn't. Now it was rolling downwards, smashing a way through the junk, picking up pace with every passing second. I knew this because I could see out of the window. Unlike Junkin' Jack and Jackie. Still flat out on the floor, all they could see was each other. And me, of course. The boy they now believed to be a magician.

'I told you there'd be consequences if you dared to cross me!' I said sternly. 'Now, get me down this instant!'

'Never!' Junkin' Jack crawled out from under his mammy and picked up the bone chopper. 'I want your fingers,' he said, climbing unsteadily to his feet. 'I want them for my Razorbacks.'

The caravan lurched suddenly to one side. We must've hit a rock, but Junkin' Jack wasn't to know that. All he could see was me waving my hands at him, almost as if I was trying to cast a spell.

'This is your final warning,' I yelled. 'Come near me again and I'll—'

I didn't get to finish my sentence as the caravan hit another bump and Junkin' Jack was sent sprawling. He crashed into the door and it swung open. Then he vanished from view altogether.

'My lovable toad!' howled Jackie. Scrambling to her feet, she rushed towards the opening in search of her son.

Bad move.

The caravan jolted and jumped. Unfortunately for Jackie, so did she. Straight out the door, in fact. Like her son, she didn't even stop to say goodbye.

With both Trashs no longer a concern, my focus switched to my ankles. The rope that Jackie had used to secure me to the ceiling had started to *groan*. It had gone beyond the fraying stage a long time ago, meaning that, any second now, it was going to ...

Snap.

I put my hands down to soften the blow, but still landed with an almighty *thud*. Before I knew it, I was sliding on my stomach towards the door. Fearful of following Junkin' Jack and Jackie, I jammed my loafers against the side table and came to a momentary halt. From where I was laid I had a clear view of outside. By the look of things, we had reached the bottom of Swill Hill and were now heading into the woodland of Back O'Beyond. I could see trees and trees and, if I really concentrated, even more trees. I knew then that the caravan was sure to hit one sooner rather than later.

Which meant that *sooner rather than later* was also the perfect time to get off.

Climbing to my feet, I shuffled over to the door and tried not to fall out by accident. I stopped in the doorway and snatched a quick breath. I would jump on three.

One ... two ...

The caravan smashed straight into a tree trunk a second later and I was thrown outside.

Too slow, Hugo. Too slow.

24.'HE'S AWAKE, FRED.'

Have you ever been thrown from an out of control caravan at an alarmingly fast speed?

No, thought not.

I have – obviously – but I wouldn't advise it. It wasn't much fun. If anything, it was absolute agony. Especially when I hit the ground with a heavy *bump* and then continued to bounce several times on my face before finally coming to a halt. And after that … well, there wasn't an after that. Not that I can remember, anyway.

The lights had gone out and I couldn't turn them back on again.

Don't panic; I'll be back soon (hopefully). Just try not to hold your breath, okay?

I was already on the move before I had even woken up. Not through choice, I might add. Laid flat on my back, with my arms above my head, I was being pulled this way and that through the ragged undergrowth by some mysterious force that was still yet to reveal itself. The experience wasn't that uncomfortable so I decided not to fight it. Not at first. Then, at some point, as the back of my head smacked against the earth for the forty-seventh time, it dawned on me that being dragged through the woods of Back O'Beyond was neither a normal occurrence nor really that enjoyable.

Not even for me.

Straining my neck, I tried to look beyond my own armpits for a better view of who was doing the dragging. All I could see, however, were leaves. They were everywhere, including all over my mystery dragger's entire body. I strained a little further and saw that the leaves ended where a pair of brown boots began. That was a relief. Trees don't tend to bother with footwear. And neither do bushes. Or man-eating plants. Or spy-gobbling shrubs …

Get a grip, Hugo.

The outline of the body looked too big to be either Junkin' Jack or Jackie, but then it looked too big to be human at all. So, what was it?

The Leafy Lugger took a sharp turn and my arms swerved violently to one side. The rest of me followed soon after, but I was too slow to prevent my knee from colliding with a tree trunk. I groaned out loud and the Leafy Lugger stopped. I didn't know what to expect to see when they turned, but a leafy face to match the leafy body was nowhere near the top of my wish list.

'I don't think we've been properly introduced,' I began. 'Or even introduced at all. No, you just decided to drag me through the woods … which, don't get me wrong, is absolutely fine … better than walking, I suppose … but sometimes it's nice to know who's doing the dragging. I'm

Pink Weasel by the way … but you can call me Pinky. And you are …?' I stopped talking and waited for an answer. Unfortunately, it never arrived. 'Don't be shy,' I said eventually. 'This is the moment you tell me your name and we become the best of buddies.'

The Leafy Lugger didn't reply, but chose, instead, to let go of my wrists. As far as I could tell we had stopped at a particularly dense section of woodland.

'No way through,' I sighed. 'Not to worry. We can always go back. Back to where you found me, I mean. Or even back to my house. I can give you directions if you like, although I can't promise I'll let you in for a cup of tea when we get there.'

Ignoring me completely, the Leafy Lugger took a step forward and pushed against the trees with equally leafy hands. To my surprise, they began to part. I looked again and realised they were actually some kind of camouflage netting. Interesting. What kind of person – if it was a person – needed a secret hideout in the woods? Not only that, but why were they so keen to show it to me?

With nothing blocking our way, the Leafy Lugger grabbed me by the wrists and set off again.

'That's clever,' I said, once we had passed through the netting. 'It's also a bit odd, but I won't hold that against you—'

I shut up suddenly as somebody else began to speak. A woman's voice, it seemed to be coming from the Leafy Lugger.

'He's awake, Fred … I know, Winnie … don't worry

about that now … concentrate on the numbers … forward two, Fred … right four … left one, Winnie … forward two … left three, Fred … forward four … right one, Winnie …'

I twisted my neck, but saw no sign of Fred or Winnie or anybody else for that matter. Nevertheless, the Leafy Lugger must have been following the commands because we kept on turning and swerving in time with every instruction.

'Up, Winnie.'

Right on cue, I felt my entire body lift up off the ground. It wasn't enough, however, to stop the back of my head from banging against something hard.

'Careful, Fred.'

Yes, be careful. I resisted the urge to shout it out loud, but then wished I had as the exact same thing happened again … and then three more times after that. It was only when the banging ended that I realised we had been climbing some steps. At least that explained the five big bruises that were now forming on the back of my head.

Raising a leg, the Leafy Lugger took aim and kicked out. One ear-splitting *crash* later and we were back on the move. Light turned to dark as I was hauled over the threshold into some kind of building. Not a house as such. No, this was more like a cabin. A cabin in the woods.

A cabin in the woods that became even darker when the door was shut behind us.

I kept completely still as the Leafy Lugger finally released her grip on me. I wanted to talk, but she beat me to it. Once again, she started to mutter to herself. And, just like before, none of what she said seemed to make much sense.

'Food? Yes, Fred … but not yet … What then, Winnie? Blanket … water … first rules of basic survival … true, Winnie, but we should question him … get to the truth … whatever it takes …'

The Leafy Lugger's mutterings became quieter and quieter as she stopped walking in circles around me and left the room. Sitting up, I took the chance to take a look around. The room was sparsely decorated with two big armchairs, a fireplace with an enormous pot beside it, ill-fitting curtains up at the window and tatty newspaper covering all four walls.

I was about to dig a little deeper when the Leafy Lugger stomped back into the room. Stopping at the fireplace, she threw a handful of something green into the pot before placing the pot on the fire.

'He thinks we haven't seen him, Winnie … looks scared, Fred … he might try and steal from us, Winnie … nothing to steal, Fred … let's feed him first … warm him up … give him strength … then kick him out, Winnie!'

The Leafy Lugger turned suddenly and threw a blanket over my face before I could get a good look at her. I pulled it off immediately; surprised to see that she had left the room again.

I had seen enough, heard enough and, most definitely, had enough.

Shifting onto my knees, I began to creep along the floorboards towards the door. I had almost made it when the fire flickered and I saw movement in the shadows. I was about to turn when something flew past my face and embedded itself in the wall.

It was an arrow.

I glanced back into the cabin and saw the Leafy Lugger stood behind me. Like before, both her face and body were completely camouflaged, but now she was carrying something.

A crossbow.

'Tell him to sit back down and get comfortable, Fred,' said the voice from somewhere within the leaves. 'He's not going anywhere, Winnie!'

25.'THERE'S NO SUCH THING AS THE RASCAL.'

The first thing I did was shuffle away from the door.

Just in case. Call me a shaken spy, but I had no idea to what lengths the Leafy Lugger would go to keep me in the cabin … and I had no wish to find out!

The second thing I did was try to plead my innocence.

'I wasn't going anywhere,' I said hastily. 'And why would I? Not when we're having such a tremendous time together.' I stopped talking and peered around the room. 'You and me … and Fred … and Winnie,' I added.

The Leafy Lugger lifted the crossbow and aimed it at my face. 'What do you know about Fred and Winnie?'

'Absolutely nothing,' I blurted out. 'No, less than that. It's just … you keep talking to them … and I can't actually see them—'

'No, I can't see them either,' the Leafy Lugger admitted. 'I am them!'

Oh dear. Of all the things she could've said that was probably the worst. Without drawing too much attention to myself, I turned back towards the door, more convinced than ever that I was better off outside rather than inside the cabin (even if I did end up minus a thumb and four fingers).

'I suppose I can't stop you from leaving if you want, Pinky.' The Leafy Lugger lowered the crossbow before finally removing the leafy mask from her head. Her face wasn't that unpleasant really. A bit wrinkly, a bit saggy around the edges, but nowhere near bad enough to hide away. Unlike her hair. That was like a badly made bird nest that had been trampled on by a herd of elephants. 'My full title is Lady Winifred Hyde,' she announced. 'I split Winifred into Winnie and Fred so I had some company. Yes, I talk to myself, but then so would you if you'd lived on your own for as long as I have.'

'I guess that makes sense,' I nodded.

'And it also makes sense for you to warm up a little and have something to eat before you go on your way,' continued Lady Hyde, gesturing towards the fireplace. 'Still, if you're not interested—'

'Oh, I'm interested.' As usual, my belly managed to speak before my brain. 'What have you got?'

Lady Hyde pointed at the pot. 'Nettle soup.'

I screwed up my face. 'No, I meant what have you got to eat?'

'Nettle soup,' repeated Lady Hyde. 'It's nicer than it sounds. Come and sit by the fire and you can try some.'

I did as she asked and fell into one of the armchairs. Before I knew it, my eyelids were beginning to close.

'What time is it?' I asked, all the while fighting the urge to nod off.

'It's still light if that helps,' said Lady Hyde, as she sat down opposite me. 'I don't have a clock or a watch or any other means of telling the time, I'm afraid. Not anymore. Not since I came to live in the woods.' Lady Hyde shrugged her shrub-covered shoulders. 'Sorry if I seem a little … unusual,' she mumbled. 'Or maybe a *lot* unusual. I'm not used to *this*.'

Now it was my turn to shrug. 'Used to what?'

'Talking,' said Lady Hyde. 'You're the first person I've spoken to in almost eleven years. You're also the first person I've seen somersaulting from a speeding caravan. That was quite peculiar. This is Back O'Beyond, though, and peculiar things do tend to happen from time to time.'

'They're happening now,' I muttered to myself. I sniffed the soup. It didn't smell of much so I took a sip. 'Not too bad,' I said, licking my lips. 'Who made it? You, Fred or Winnie?'

'Ha! Very funny,' smiled Lady Hyde. 'It was all three of us actually.'

'It must be quite a squeeze at times,' I joked. 'Especially in a cabin this size. Still, if it's all you can afford—'

'Oh, I can afford much more than this,' replied Lady Hyde matter-of-factly. 'I've got lots of money. I'm arguably richer than the whole of Crooked Elbow and Twisted Kneecap put together. I was born into wealth and it's followed me around all my life.'

'And yet you choose to eat nettle soup,' I remarked.

'No, I choose to live off the earth,' Lady Hyde argued. 'I don't go to the shops and I refuse to buy food. I grow everything I eat. It's a simple way of life, but I have no worries or concerns … until you showed up!'

'I've been called worse,' I said. 'Thanks for coming to my rescue, though. You must be as strong as an ox to drag me through the woods.'

A wide grin spread across Lady Hyde's lips. 'I've had to be strong. I've done a lot in my life and most of it has been quite extreme. I've been an explorer … a deep sea diver … a racing driver … a trapeze artist … a stunt woman … and, perhaps most importantly of all, a spy.'

'A spy?' I repeated.

'A spy,' nodded Lady Hyde. 'And, unless I'm sorely mistaken, that's something we've both got in common.'

My jaw dropped, but it wasn't enough to stop me from speaking (or continuing to eat for that matter). 'How did you know?'

'I can spot a spy a mile off,' explained Lady Hyde. 'Although it is easier to spot one when they're sat directly opposite me. Don't get me wrong: I was a spy a long, long time ago. Before you were born, in fact. At a guess, I wasn't much older than you when I first started working for SICK. My codename was Burgundy Bear. I was Agent Two. Never did make it to Agent One, though.'

'Agent Two?' I tried not to think about my own number, but then tried even harder not to say it out loud by accident. 'Yeah, I could've been Agent Two,' I said, shifting awkwardly in the armchair. 'Turned it down … too obvious … shall we move on?'

'I did most things when I was a spy,' continued Lady

Hyde, deep in thought, 'although nothing quite as bizarre as being tossed from a runaway caravan. Would you care to explain?'

'I don't think you'd believe me even if I tried,' I said. 'To cut a long story short, it was the result of spending all day searching for the Rascal.'

Lady Hyde snorted with so much force that the fire almost went out. 'You could search all year, but you'd never succeed,' she said bluntly. 'There's no such thing as the Rascal. It's a myth. A legend. A story that's grown and grown over time, but has nothing to back it up.'

'That's where you're wrong,' I argued. 'The Rascal's been communicating with me all day. Sending me scrolls telling me where to find him.'

'Yes, because that would be a great idea, wouldn't it?' Lady Hyde shook her bird nest at me in disgust. 'Somebody might have been sending you notes, Pinky, but it wasn't the Rascal. I mean, have you seen him yet?'

'Nearly … but not quite,' I muttered. 'Or just not at all. I keep on missing him.'

'That's convenient,' sighed Lady Hyde. 'You're a spy now, Pinky, so you must strive to think like one. Listen and learn. Things aren't always what they seem. Sometimes you have to take a step back to see where you're heading. Try to ignore the obvious and concentrate on the obscure. Remember, your brain is your most powerful weapon. What are you thinking about now for example?'

'I'm thinking about another bowl of nettle soup,' I said honestly. Lady Hyde was about to oblige when, out of the blue, a high-pitched bell started to ring out around the cabin. 'What's going on?' I cried, clamping my hands over my ears.

'We're under attack.' Lady Hyde shot up from the armchair and hurried over to the window. 'That's my alarm you can hear,' she said, peeking through the curtains. 'I've got sensors outside placed strategically all around the cabin. One of them must have been triggered.'

'What does that mean?' I asked.

'It means there's somebody in the woods,' revealed Lady Hyde. 'They can't be friendly because I haven't got any. Friends, I mean. Enemies, however, are a different matter altogether. I've got lots of those. And it wouldn't surprise me if you did, too.'

'That's true,' I had to admit. 'So, what do we do now?'

'We wait.' Lady Hyde moved away from the window. 'They can try to get in,' she said, picking up the crossbow, 'but I can assure you they won't get out alive!'

26.'YOU'RE NOT WELCOME HERE!'

Lady Hyde pulled open the door to the cabin and stepped outside.

'I've got traps set up all over the woods,' she admitted. 'There are at least forty-three of them dotted about. Impossible to avoid unless you know exactly where they are.'

'Is that why you were counting out loud and moving from left to right when you dragged me here?' I asked.

'Indeed,' nodded Lady Hyde. 'An intruder would stand no chance of dodging all those pitfalls. We'll find out for sure soon enough ... once the screaming starts!'

'Nice,' I said, wincing at the thought of it. 'What sort of traps are there?'

'Hmm, let me see.' Lady Hyde ran a hand through her bird-nest hair. 'There are holes filled with sludge ... holes filled with spikes ... holes filled with sludge and spikes ... giant mousetraps designed to trap a human ... male or female, I'm not fussy ... nets coming down from trees ... nets coming up from under bushes ... and ... and ... and something else I can't quite—'

Lady Hyde stopped mid-sentence as a loud *boom* shook the cabin.

'Ah, that's it,' she said, as smoke rose up through the trees. 'I've hidden explosives under the surface of the earth. I think our intruder might have just stepped on one.'

'Sounds painful,' I muttered.

'Hopefully.' Lady Hyde crouched down and lifted the crossbow to her eye. 'Get behind me, Pinky,' she said firmly. 'When I see the intruder coming up the garden, I'll pick them off with an arrow.'

'Are you sure that's wise?' I frowned. 'It could be anyone.'

'I know it could,' agreed Lady Hyde. 'It could be anyone who should know better than to walk onto my property. Now stop standing there and get down. The intruder might be armed.'

I reluctantly did as she asked. The smoke from the first explosion had drifted away and I half-expected another trap to be activated when …

'Arrggghhh!'

The scream echoed around the woods for fourteen long seconds. When it finally stopped, I could hear Lady Hyde giggling to herself.

'I think our intruder may have fallen over a trip wire,' she said excitedly. 'Which probably means—'

'Urrggghhhh!'

'They've also walked straight into a tree,' finished Lady Hyde. 'I use mirrors to conceal them. Very clever, even if I say so myself.'

'Clever *and* sneaky,' I added.

'The perfect combination,' said Lady Hyde. As she spoke a figure emerged from out of the woods. They were small in height and dressed entirely in black. Or rather, they were *almost* dressed in black. Now their clothes were ripped all over and covered in mud and grass stains. Moving clumsily from tree to tree, they seemed to be limping badly whilst one arm was hanging awkwardly by their side, no doubt the result of walking unknowingly into all those traps.

'Target identified,' whispered Lady Hyde. 'Can you see them, Pinky?'

'No,' I lied. 'I can't see anyone. There's definitely nobody stumbling through your garden—'

'There.' Lady Hyde tensed up as the figure stepped out into the open. 'You can't miss them now … and neither can I!'

She wasn't wrong. The figure had stopped creeping about and was now in full view as they made their way towards the cabin.

To my horror, I knew who it was.

'Don't shoot!' I cried.

'Too late,' said Lady Hyde. At the same time, she pulled the trigger, the crossbow jerked and the arrow flew towards the intruder.

The intruder I now knew to be Agent Sixteen. Violet Crow. My SICK sister.

I tried to shout a warning. I wanted to tell Crow to duck, dive or dodge, but, in the end, the words couldn't escape from my mouth quick enough.

And, in hindsight, it was a good job they didn't.

Hobbling along, Crow was moving so slowly that the arrow fell short and missed her by a matter of inches. She must have sensed something because she looked up almost immediately. I waved her away, but she didn't seem to understand and kept on coming.

'Bad luck, Fred ... must try harder, Winnie,' muttered Lady Hyde under her breath. Reaching inside her pouch, she grabbed another arrow and slotted it into the crossbow.

'No, don't try at all,' I blurted out.

Lady Hyde ignored me as she lined up another shot.

Rather than turning on her heels, Violet Crow did the exact opposite and continued to cross the garden. She was getting closer with every step.

So close, in fact, that I doubted Lady Hyde would miss again.

I had to do something. Something that hopefully didn't involve me getting hurt. So not something like standing in front of Lady Hyde to stop her from firing. No way. Definitely not. That would've just been ridiculous.

Without thinking, I stood up and moved in front of Lady Hyde to stop her from firing.

'What are you doing, Pinky?' she cried.

'Being a nuisance,' I said nervously. 'It's what I do best. This time, however, there's a good reason for it. I don't want you to shoot. Not at her. And certainly not at me.'

Lady Hyde took a moment to think before she lowered the crossbow. 'Who is she?'

'She's SICK,' I explained. 'Her codename is Violet Crow. You can trust her.'

'I'm not sure I can,' remarked Lady Hyde. 'And neither can you. There's something about her I don't like.' Lady

Hyde switched her attention to Agent Sixteen. 'What do you want?' she called out.

'Just Pink Weasel,' replied Crow, pointing towards me. 'Nothing else. But I'm not leaving without him.'

'You're not welcome here,' insisted Lady Hyde.

'Oh, you don't say!' Violet Crow bent down and retrieved the arrow that had landed by her feet. 'I'm not sure this is the best way to greet a visitor,' she said coldly. 'Now, if you would be so kind – if that's possible – I'd like to speak to Pink Weasel … in private. What I have to say isn't for your ears.'

Lady Hyde lifted the crossbow. 'How dare you!'

'I dare because it's important,' shot back Crow. 'Important to everyone in Crooked Elbow. Important to everyone in Twisted Kneecap. It's even important to you, you mouldy old fossil. Just hurry up and send Pink Weasel to me otherwise we'll all suffer.'

'I should probably go,' I said.

'It's your choice,' shrugged Lady Hyde. 'The *wrong* choice, of course, but we all have to learn from our mistakes.'

I was halfway down the steps when a horrible thought crossed my mind. 'There aren't any traps around here, are there?' I asked warily.

'Of course not,' said Lady Hyde, shaking her head. 'I mean, probably not … there could be, I suppose … possibly … maybe. I've had an idea. Just close your eyes, cross your fingers and hope for the best. I'm sure you'll be fine.'

So that was what I did. Kind of. Unfortunately, I crossed my legs instead of my fingers and stumbled down the last few steps.

'Get up, Weasel,' groaned Crow, as I landed beside her. 'You're embarrassing yourself.'

'Not for the first time,' I admitted. 'I embarrass myself at least seventeen times a day. Sometimes more if I forget to get dressed in the morning.' I climbed up off the grass and brushed myself down. 'What are you doing here anyway?'

'Looking for you,' scowled Crow. 'And, trust me, it wasn't easy. Still, I'm here now. *Just*. This is for you.' Crow passed me a scroll. 'I found it in the woods,' she revealed. 'I'm guessing this is like the others you've been reading all day.'

I smiled as I took it from her and then did just that.

To the spy who seeks me,

Oh, this is even more awkward than last time. I only said you'd find a Rascal at Junkin' Jack's Scrap Shack – not the Rascal. Now, please pay attention because you keep on getting things wrong. Your next destination is the Wonderful World of Warehouses. Look hard enough and you'll find me in the one marked M.T.

Until we finally meet, the Rascal.

I was about to read it for a second time when Violet Crow snatched the scroll from out of my grasp.

'You don't believe this nonsense, do you?' she frowned.

'Why wouldn't I?' I shot back. 'And, even if I didn't, what other choice do I have? None. That's the answer. And that's why I'm going to the Wonderful World of

Warehouses. Let me spell it out for you, Crow.' I hesitated. 'No, I'll just say it. It's easier that way. Basically, I'm going to end this once and for all. I'm going to catch the Rascal. And nothing is going to stop me.'

And that was the exact moment I puffed out my chest, turned back towards the cabin and stepped on one of Lady Hyde's traps.

Whoops.

27.'I NEVER ASKED YOU TO RESCUE ME.'

It didn't hurt.

Not much anyway.

Okay, so it hurt enough to make my eyes water and my nose run, but not enough to put me out of action.

Yes, it hurt enough for Lady Winifred Hyde to lead us through the rest of her traps into the relative safety of Back O'Beyond, but not enough to stop me from feeling just a little bit embarrassed that she had to hold my hand whilst she did so.

Turns out there were more traps than she remembered. At least eighty-three at last count. And that's not including the four that my good self and Violet Crow had accidentally stepped on or walked into.

Safe and sound and still in something resembling one piece, I was about to leave Lady Hyde to her nettle-collecting when she grabbed me by the elbow. Violet Crow stopped too, but Lady Hyde was quick to wave her away. 'Be careful out there, Pinky,' she whispered. 'I've a bad feeling that danger may be just around the corner.'

'If that's the case, I'll walk in a straight line,' I said smartly.

'That's not what I meant,' sighed Lady Hyde. 'Sometimes you have to bend and swerve just to stay alive. Remember though, Pinky, whatever happens there will always be a pot of nettle soup waiting for you on the fire.'

I bid my new foliage-faced friend a fond farewell and then set off after Violet Crow, who had stubbornly carried on alone through the woods. Two trips, three stumbles and four falls later, I finally caught up with her.

'I have transport,' she remarked. 'I can take you to the Wonderful World of Warehouses … if that's what you want.'

'I want, but why would you?' I replied. 'In fact, why are you doing any of this? It's not as if you want me to catch the Rascal. Not before you, anyway.'

'Listen.' Crow spun around and poked me on the forehead. 'Stop asking questions, Weasel, and start being grateful that I keep on coming to your rescue.'

'I never asked you to rescue me,' I said. 'Half the time I'm not even in any danger.'

'No, but you could've been,' argued Crow. 'Whatever I think of you – and that's not much if I'm being honest – you're still a spy. And so am I. We work for SICK. We stick together. Right?'

I shrugged in agreement. Maybe she had a point and I was just being awkward for the sake of it.

Still, that didn't stop me from being awkward for the sake of it just a little bit more.

'Lady Hyde didn't seem to particularly like you,' I said matter-of-factly.

'Who? That sour old stuffing ball with the big leafy coat and the even bigger chip on her shoulder?' remarked Crow. 'Well, guess what? I don't like her either!'

I slipped through a gap in the trees and spotted a wooden fence in the distance. By the look of things we had reached the edge of Back O'Beyond. 'She said she didn't trust you,' I continued.

'Good for her,' muttered Crow, as she beat her way through the bushes. 'She means nothing to me. Less than nothing. If you hadn't brought her up I would probably have forgotten that she even existed by now. Oh, who are we talking about again? No, I don't know her.'

Violet Crow reached the fence before me and vaulted over it without breaking stride. I tried to follow her lead, but something went badly wrong. My foot got caught in the middle panel, my hand slipped and my body fell forward. I was inches away from landing face-first on the ground when Crow grabbed me by my waistcoat and put me safely back on my feet.

'I thought you didn't need rescuing,' she said, stern-faced.

'Maybe just once in a while,' I had to admit. 'Or twice every few minutes. Or three times in a—'

'Just get in!' ordered Crow.

'Get in?' I looked around. We were stood on the side of a narrow path that was barely wide enough for a single vehicle. There was no traffic coming from either direction or nothing parked up on the roadside.

Nothing except for an antique motorcycle and rickety sidecar.

'Not that,' I said, laughing nervously.

'Yes, that,' said Crow, as she climbed onto the motorcycle. 'Now get in the sidecar before I change my mind and leave you here.'

'I think I'd prefer that,' I muttered.

'What do you mean?' Crow picked up a helmet and pulled it over her spiky head. 'This vehicle is perfectly safe.'

'About ninety-nine years ago perhaps,' I grumbled. 'These days, however …'

'It's as good as it gets,' spat Crow, finishing my sentence. 'We both know that you're going to get in the sidecar eventually, Weasel, so just hurry up about it. You really are quite predictable sometimes.'

'I'm anything but predictable,' I insisted. A moment later I predictably clambered into the sidecar, just like Crow had said. It wasn't as large as I had hoped, but if I pressed my knees up to my chin and rested my ears on my shoulders I could just about squeeze in.

'This is the long and winding road to Crooked Elbow,' said Crow, as she strapped on her goggles. 'Other vehicles don't come this way because it's so twisty-turny and far too bumpy for anyone with even half a brain to travel on.'

'Is that why we're using it?' I asked.

'It's also the safest way for us to get to the Wonderful World of Warehouses without being spotted,' explained Crow. The sidecar shook as she turned the key and revved the engine. 'Now, just hold on tight and try not to breathe unless it's absolutely necessary,' Crow instructed. 'And, whatever you do, don't tell me to slow down. That just makes things worse.'

I tensed up as the motorcycle jerked forward. 'Oh, I almost forgot,' said Crow, stopping suddenly. Leaning across, she handed me another helmet and a pair of goggles. 'You'll need these,' she said. 'Especially if you fall out.'

'Fall out?' I quickly put them on as the motorcycle jerked forward for a second time. 'What do you mean *if I fall out?*' I cried.

'My mistake,' yelled Crow, as we shot off along the long and winding road. 'I meant *when* you fall out!'

I didn't.

Fall out, I mean.

I jumped, jarred, jolted, and jiggled about a bit, but somehow, against all the odds, my bottom stayed firmly rooted inside the sidecar. As she had suggested, Violet Crow rode at a rapid rate, which, if nothing else, at least made our journey shorter than expected. At last count it took a little over one thousand seconds. Give or take. I stopped at twenty-seven so I can't really be certain.

I pulled off the goggles and then weighed up whether or not to be sick in the helmet before I took my first look at the Wonderful World of Warehouses. It was exactly what you'd imagine. Without the wonderful bit, of course. That was definitely false advertising. Oh, and the world bit wasn't strictly true either. No way was it that big. Not even close.

Simply put, the Wonderful World of Warehouses was just a lot of very large buildings in a very large area. Quite boring really, even for the most fanatical of warehouse fans.

'We need to find the one marked *M.T.*,' I said, stepping out of the sidecar. A moment later I collapsed in a heap. My legs had gone so numb during the journey that I couldn't even take my own weight.

'You mean the empty one?' said Crow, as she swung a leg and climbed off the motorcycle.

'No, the *M.T.* one,' I argued. 'There's a big difference. Now, are you going to help me up or not?'

'I'll help you up, but that's all.' Crow dragged me to my feet and then held me there until I regained my strength. 'I'm not searching for any warehouse,' she said bluntly. 'I just provided the transport.'

'But you said … I thought … we were …' None of that made any sense, not even to me. 'You read the scroll,' I insisted. 'We know where the Rascal is. We can catch him together.'

'That won't happen,' said Crow, shaking her helmet as she got back onto the motorcycle. 'Not here. Not now. Not ever. You're wasting your time, Weasel … but I won't be wasting mine!'

With that, Violet Crow started the engine and rode off before I had a chance to say goodbye. I watched as she weaved in and out of numerous not-so-wonderful warehouses before accelerating fast. Then she was gone.

The warehouses that surrounded me were all collosal in size, grey in colour and ugly in appearance. And, at first glance at least, identical in every way imaginable. With little option but to walk between them, I set my eyes to red alert for any sign of the *M.T.* that would identify the one I was searching for.

Seventy-three warehouses later and I had drawn a blank.

I struck lucky, however, on the seventy-fourth. With its sliding door pulled ever-so-slightly to one side, I crept towards that particular warehouse, wary of what might be lurking in the doorway. Then I spotted it. Painted on the side in black.

M.T.

This was the one. If I believed the Rascal then he was inside, ready and waiting.

And, three steps later, so was I.

28.'WE'RE NOT ALONE.'

The M.T. warehouse was just that.

Empty.

And dark. Very dark. Okay, not completely *can't-see-a-thing* dark, but even if I squinted with one eye and strained with the other I still couldn't quite make out what was curled up in all four corners or swinging from the ceiling. If the Rascal was hiding then they were the only places he could be.

Unlike me.

I was in full view and completely exposed as I paused in the doorway. That was something I had to change. And fast.

My first move was to slide the door across until it was tightly shut. Now it really was *can't-see-a-thing* dark in the warehouse. Yes, it was a risky move and, yes, I had blocked off my only means of escape, but it also meant that the Rascal couldn't escape either.

If this was a trap then at least we would be trapped in here together.

Tiptoeing to my right, I pressed my back against the wall before carefully removing the walking stick from my trousers. I placed it down by my feet and used it to lead the way as I moved slowly towards the first corner of the warehouse. Nerves got the better of my legs and I began to speed up. Even though I knew that the walking stick would get there before me and strike the opposite wall, I still wasn't ready when it happened.

And that was why I dropped it.

The walking stick made a horrible clattering sound as it landed on the warehouse floor. I held my breath as the noise echoed for what seemed like an eternity. Or just eleven seconds. I'll let you decide which is closer to the truth.

It was only when I crouched down to pick it up that I saw a beam of light coming from another corner of the warehouse. I stayed low as it bounced from wall to wall without ever actually landing directly on me.

'Who's there? … Who's there? … Who's there?'

It was a man's voice. He only spoke once, but like the falling walking stick, his question echoed repeatedly.

'Come out … come out … come out.'

I watched as the light drew closer to where I was crouched. Springing to my feet, I swerved to one side and then began to run back the way I had just come. I figured it was best to stay on the move; my pounding footsteps a perfect distraction for anybody listening out for the slightest of sounds. I chose not to leave via the sliding door and continued to run around the perimeter of the warehouse instead. Satisfied that I had well and truly confused whoever was in there with me, I slammed on my foot brakes and came to a skidding halt.

'This is the end,' I called out. 'I'm here to put a stop to your little games.'

There was a loud snort before the voice replied. 'I'm not the one playing games – you are!'

'No, I'm not,' I argued. 'I'm deadly serious. And seriously deadly so you'd better watch out.'

As expected, the beam of light rested on the corner I had only just vacated. I had out run it; which meant whoever was doing the shining had no idea where I was. If I made my move now I could catch him unawares.

If only it was that easy …

I was all set to shift when the light swung around and hit me straight between the eyes. I was blinded.

'That's my waistcoat.'

That one sentence was enough to stop me in my tracks. It also revealed two things. Not only was the man in the corner of the warehouse more than familiar with my clothing, but, all of a sudden, I knew who he was.

'You?' I said, shielding my eyes.

'Yes, me.' I watched as the Chief of SICK himself, the Big Cheese, turned the light under his own chin. With his bald head, droopy moustache and huge teeth, his face was both exactly how I remembered it and incredibly spooky at the same time. 'And you're you, young Dare,' he added. 'Pink Weasel. Agent Minus Thirty-Five. Or that was what I used to think. Now, however, I'm not so sure.'

'Well, I'm sure,' I remarked. 'And I'm also sure that you shouldn't be here … unless … no, surely not …' I drew a breath, barely able to believe what I was about to say. 'You're the Rascal!'

'Me?' The Big Cheese spoke so loudly that my eardrums began to vibrate. 'Think again, you mumbling monkfish!' he boomed. 'I'm no such thing. You, though, *are* such a thing. You're the Rascal. I would never have believed it—'

'You don't have to, sir,' I said, butting in. 'Because I'm not.'

'But you must be,' the Big Cheese insisted. 'Otherwise you wouldn't be in this warehouse.'

'I could say the same thing about you,' I replied. 'So I will. The Rascal sent me a scroll saying he'd meet me here.'

'Me too.' The Big Cheese marched towards me waving a paper scroll identical to those I had been following all day. 'It said I would find the Rascal in the *M.T.* warehouse,' he revealed. 'So here I am. And here are you.' The light hopped about as the Big Cheese tapped the torch against his forehead. 'Do you know what I'm thinking?' he said.

I swallowed nervously. 'You think that we've both been tricked and this is a trap and any minute now the Rascal is going to pop up and finish us off.'

'Not even close!' bellowed the Big Cheese. 'I was actually thinking that this might all be a dream and you're not really here and neither am I and very soon I'll wake up with my head on my pillow and my thumb in my mouth and … ugh!'

The Chief of SICK stopped mid-sentence. And not through choice. Much to his obvious displeasure I had put my hand over his mouth to stop him from talking.

And that was because I had heard something.

It was coming from the other side of the warehouse.

'We're not alone,' I said, slowly removing my hand.

'Of course we're not,' cried the Big Cheese. 'We've got each other. Just the two of us … ugh!'

Once again, the Chief of SICK had to be silenced. This time, however, I used my elbow to fill the hole. 'Listen,' I said quietly.

Against his better judgement, the Big Cheese did as I asked. A few seconds later his moustache began to twitch. He had heard it, too. Soft footsteps and rustling clothes. Heavy breathing and the occasional snort.

'The Rascal,' said the Big Cheese quietly.

'The Rascal,' I said, nodding in agreement.

I tried to follow the sounds, but couldn't see a thing. The Rascal – if that's who it was – must've been lurking in one of the corners all the time we had been in the warehouse. We, however, were now stood out in the open. Easy targets from every angle.

The Big Cheese must have realised this at the same time as me as he stuck his torch down the front of his trousers. He could've just switched it off I suppose, but what would be the fun in that.

'Some people say the best form of defence is attack,' he began, 'but I'm not one of those people. I prefer to play hide and seek … especially when I'm the one who's hiding!'

To my surprise, the Big Cheese disappeared from my side. He hadn't gone far, though. 'Why have you sat down?' I asked.

'This is the best hiding place I could think of,' he explained. 'If I close my eyes it'll be even better. Perfectly safe.'

I left the Big Cheese to it and made my way across the warehouse. This was our best chance of catching the Rascal. I couldn't let it go to waste.

I had barely moved when I heard a flurry of scampering footsteps followed by a *thwack* and a *thud* and a high-pitched scream. Before I knew it, there was something tight around my neck. I tried to pull it away, but it held firm.

The footsteps faded and the screaming stopped, only to be replaced by a loud *cracking* sound as the warehouse was suddenly illuminated. The lights were on. Why hadn't I thought of that when I had first entered? Things would've been a whole lot easier if I had. I would've been able to see for a start.

Just like now, in fact..

Now I could see that the amount of people in the warehouse had doubled from two to four.

One was me.

One was the Big Cheese.

And the other two were neither of us. They were completely different people. One of whom had to be the Rascal.

Didn't they?

29.'DON'T BREATHE!'

I knew the other two people in the warehouse like the back of my head.

Not very well at all.

But I had met them both already that day … and it hadn't ended well.

One of them was 'Diamond' Duke Majestic. Towering over me like a smartly-dressed lamppost, it was his hand that was around my throat (and, as far as I could tell, it wasn't intended as a friendly greeting).

The other person was Detective Inspector Spite. He was closer to the Big Cheese than me. So close, in fact, that his megaphone was rubbing up against the Chief of SICK's ear.

'We are the police!' Spite hollered.

'No, we are not,' moaned the Big Cheese, pushing the megaphone away as he climbed to his feet. 'You are the police. Just you and you only. And as for you …' The Big Cheese pointed at Diamond Duke. 'You're nothing but a devious diamond smuggler. And devious diamond smugglers should not have their hands around one of my agent's throats.'

'Why not?' As if to prove his point, Duke lifted me off

the ground until I was hanging in mid-air.

'Why not?' repeated the Big Cheese. 'I thought that would've been obvious. It's unhygienic for a start. You don't know where he's been.'

'I know exactly where he's been,' argued Duke, as he tightened his grip. 'He's been on my train. He led the police straight to us and we lost our diamonds. He keeps on doing that!' Duke stopped suddenly. 'One of your agents?' he said, confused. 'But that would make him a … spy?'

'Indeed he is,' nodded the Big Cheese. 'I know it's hard to believe—'

'It's harder than that,' muttered Duke.

'It's impossible,' agreed Spite.

'I'm not that bad.' It wasn't easy to speak with Diamond Duke's hands around my neck, but I felt obliged to defend myself. 'I'm actually quite good. Well, better than average. That's right, isn't it, sir?'

I looked towards the Big Cheese for reassurance, but it wasn't forthcoming.

'Shall we just get back to the matter at hand?' he muttered eventually.

'The matter at hand is me arresting Duke Majestic,' remarked Spite eagerly. 'He got lucky back on that train and managed to slip away from me. That luck, however, has just run out. I was told I would find you in this warehouse, Duke, and here you are.'

'Well, I was told Pink Weasel would be here,' shot back Duke. 'And here he is … alive and kicking … but not for much longer!'

'Stop this nonsense right now!' boomed the Big Cheese, stamping his foot in anger. 'This isn't supposed to be happening. Pink Weasel and I are here for the Rascal. Nobody else. It says so on our scrolls—'

'I got a scroll,' revealed Duke. 'I found it in the woods of Back O'Beyond after I had managed to dodge the police for the seventh time this week—'

'Sixth time,' argued Spite.

'Same difference,' shrugged Duke. 'I don't know where the scroll came from, but it was addressed to me. It was from the Rascal. He said he had something I wanted … here in the *M.T.* warehouse … and that something was Pink Weasel.'

The same thing happened to me,' said Spite, 'but the Rascal told me I could get my hands on both Duke and Pink Weasel.' Spite stopped and jabbed his megaphone in my direction. 'Although none of that actually makes sense because you tried to tell me you were the Rascal,' he added.

'Did I?' I replied awkwardly. 'Oh, yes, so I did. It was back at Mysterious Melvin's Museum of Mind-Bending Marvels, wasn't it? It seemed like a good idea at the time, but I can't remember why. In fact, I can't remember anything … and I can barely speak … and my eyes are starting to blur … and … and …'

'Put him down, Duke,' suggested Spite. 'Before he passes out.'

To my relief, Diamond Duke did the decent thing and finally let go of my throat. I landed heavily, took a deep breath and then decided to take another because one clearly wasn't enough. 'Contrary to what I told you earlier, Spite, I am not the Rascal,' I said honestly. 'Never have been, never will be. So, which one of you is?'

'Don't look at me,' cried the Big Cheese.

'Or me,' frowned Spite.

'And definitely not at me,' said a stern-faced Duke Majestic.

'They'll be nowhere left to look at this rate.' I took a moment to weigh things up. 'I don't think the Rascal is any of us,' I said eventually.

'And I don't think you're wrong,' nodded the Big Cheese. 'But, if that's the case, then what's going on? Why are we all here? And … why is there smoke coming in through the air vent?'

Nobody answered. Not because they didn't want to, but because they were all far too busy looking up at the ceiling. Unfortunately, the Big Cheese wasn't mistaken; there was smoke streaming into the warehouse.

'It might be poisonous,' cried a panic-stricken Big Cheese. 'Don't breathe!'

'What? Never?' I said, screwing up my face.

'Not until we get out,' insisted Spite. Without another word, he hurried towards the exit. 'Me first,' he said, pulling at the sliding door. 'I'll just … I can't seem to … it won't budge …'

'Move!' Diamond Duke shoved him to one side so he could grab the door handle with both hands. The result, however, was the same. Try as he might, he couldn't get it to open.

'I think it might be locked,' I said.

'I *know* it might be locked,' replied the Big Cheese. 'And doors don't tend to lock themselves by accident. Somebody has trapped us all in here on purpose. Like peas in a pod. Crisps in a crisp packet. Sausages in a … erm … sausage factory.'

'And now they're going to do what?' I wondered, not entirely convinced. 'Eat us?'

'No, poison us,' remarked Spite.

Not for the first time we all looked up at the ceiling. The smoke that had entered through the vent was hovering above us like a raincloud ready to burst.

'You haven't been breathing, have you?' asked the Big Cheese. 'I did warn you.'

Yes, he did. And, by the look of things, it wasn't just me who had struggled to follow such simple instructions.

Being the tallest, Diamond Duke was the first to drop. As a last resort, he grabbed his cane and tried to waft the smoke away, but it wasn't enough to stop him from sinking to his knees and falling face-first onto the floor of the warehouse.

Detective Inspector Spite was next. Not even his megaphone could stop his legs from crumpling as he toppled backwards like a human domino. I thought about catching him, but then decided against it. It was nothing personal, of course (it was).

And then there were two …

The Big Cheese looked unsteady on his feet. Very wobbly.

'Who's doing this?' I muttered through gritted teeth.

'I think we both know the answer to that,' mumbled the Big Cheese. 'It's the ... the ...'

His sentence collapsed at the same time as his body. Fortunately, he went down slowly. Quite graceful, in fact. No cracks or crumbles. No snaps or splits. By the time he had finished he was curled up in a ball with his knees up to his chin. The lights were still on in the warehouse, but the same couldn't be said about the Big Cheese.

'The Rascal,' I whispered. It seemed hard to believe, but that mischievous monkey had set a trap and we had all willingly walked into it.

It was over.

Almost.

There was still one man standing. No, one *spy* standing. Maybe I could still stop the Rascal. All I had to do was get out of the warehouse and I could start again.

This time, however, I would do things differently.

All day long I had followed the instructions on the scrolls without really thinking. That was my mistake. If I was going to catch the Rascal then I would have to start thinking like him. Lady Hyde had told me that. Maybe she was right. Maybe she was right about other things as well. And other people.

My head felt woozy and my eyes had glazed over. I could tell that my legs were about to fold like paper. My last thought was to sit down before I fell down.

That was good thinking on my part because a second after that the smoke drifted up my nostrils and I collapsed.

No more last spy standing.

No more Pink Weasel.

No … more.

30.'YOU'RE ALIVE!'

I didn't know for certain that I was going to wake up.

As far as I was concerned, that could've been it. The grand finale. The end of Hugo Dare. Poisoned in a warehouse whilst searching for the Rascal. What a way to go!

Thankfully, it wasn't. The end, I mean. Which is good news for both me *and* you because just imagine how boring the rest of this book would be without me in it (it's not that great as it is. Surely it could've been a little more exciting. And funny. And what about the pictures? Everybody likes pictures. Why aren't there any pictures?)

When I did eventually wake I was slumped against what can only be described as a wall. Well, it was cold and flat and vertical. That was good enough for me.

My eyes were open, but I couldn't see a thing. So, I was blind. Brilliant. It came as even more of a shock when I lifted my hands to my face and found that my eyes weren't even there. They seemed to have vanished. Disappeared in a blink of an … no, that doesn't work. Not anymore.

That was my first thought anyway; that my eyes had gone. My second was that there was something covering them, obscuring my view.

Something like a blindfold.

I removed it in a flash. That was better. My eyes may not have deserted me, but I still had to blink several times and wait for them to adjust before I could make out my new surroundings. Wherever we were, it was dark and gloomy. I spotted the Big Cheese sat beside me, his back against the wall, his own eyes covered with a blindfold. I nudged him, but he didn't move. Not good. Either he was still out cold or just out for good.

My focus shifted to the other side of the room. There was a man stood in the shadows. He was wearing a long coat and a trilby hat that concealed his features.

Oh, and he was carrying a gun. It was pointing across the room.

Straight at me and the Big Cheese.

Does any of this sound familiar? Because it should do. This, dear reader, was where we first met. Where my story began. All those pages ago. Way, way back in the prologue.

I nudged the Big Cheese for a second time. And a third time. And a fourth time. Then I elbowed him in the ribs because gently nudging him didn't appear to be getting me anywhere.

Ah, that seemed to do the trick.

Wide awake, a panic-stricken Big Cheese followed my lead and pulled the blindfold from his face. We talked a little, just boring stuff (you can look back in the prologue if you don't believe me). Then I tried to get serious.

'I've been here before, sir,' I remarked, my eyes drifting

around the room. 'And I don't think we've got anything to be afraid of.'

'No, not much,' groaned the Big Cheese. 'Only the man with the pointed gun. Still, there's only one way to find out for sure if he's the dreaded Rascal we've been searching for …' The Big Cheese took a huge breath. 'Are you the dreaded Rascal we've been searching for?' he bellowed at the top of his voice.

'Why don't you speak up a little, sir?' I moaned. 'I'm sure there's one person on the other side of Crooked Elbow who didn't quite hear you the first time.'

'Zip it, young Dare,' growled the Big Cheese. 'I think the Rascal is about to answer.'

He didn't.

Not only that, but he didn't move. Not in the slightest. Not even a flicker or a flinch. A shuffle or a sway. A blink of the belly button or a tap of the toenails. In fact, as far as I could tell, he wasn't even breathing.

'He's a dummy,' I blurted out.

'Bit rude,' mumbled the Big Cheese. 'We don't want to upset him.'

'You can't upset something that can't hear you,' I explained. 'And that dummy can't hear me because he hasn't got any ears. Or eyes. Or a nose. He's not real. He's straight out of a shop window. Let me prove it—'

'Permission denied!' cried the Big Cheese, as I clambered to my feet. 'I know exactly what you're going to do … and I'm ordering you not to!'

'Oh, don't be like that,' I said. 'We're not going to get

shot. No way. Not on your nelly. I'm one-hundred-and-eighteen-per-cent certain of it. Sometimes you've just got to trust me.'

'Young Dare …' warned the Big Cheese.

I was halfway across the room when the Chief of SICK jumped up and tried to grab my arm. At the same time there was a loud *crack*.

I turned in horror as the Big Cheese slumped to the ground, clutching his chest.

Whoops.

That wasn't supposed to happen.

The Big Cheese had been shot … and it was all my fault!

Or maybe not.

I took another step forward, but this time nothing happened. There was no flash of light. No loud crack. No second shot.

Wary of any sudden movements, I carefully removed the walking stick from my trousers and let it gradually extend until it was long enough to reach the opposite wall. That was when I used it to press down on the light switch.

I was right. The man with the pointed gun wasn't the Rascal. He wasn't even a man. He was a dummy, just like the last time I had been here. And the gun? That was nothing more than a water pistol.

And yet somehow, for some unknown reason, the Big Cheese was still laid out on the floor.

I rushed over and rolled him onto his back. His eyes were closed, but he was still breathing.

And groaning.

And moaning.

And definitely not dying.

'You're alive!' I said.

'Apparently so.' A tear ran down the big Cheese's cheek as he slowly opened his eyes. 'It's a miracle,' he gushed. 'Although I do think you need to get me to a hospital …'

'Why?' I gave him a quick once over, but couldn't see anything out of the ordinary. 'What's wrong? You haven't been shot—'

'No, not shot,' agreed the Big Cheese. He tried to sit up, but failed tragically. 'This is far worse than being shot.'

'Tell me,' I said. 'I might be able to help.'

The Big Cheese waved me away. 'I'm beyond help,' he replied. 'I'm not ashamed to admit it, young Dare, but I panicked … when you moved towards the Rascal—'

'The dummy,' I said, correcting him.

'The dummy that I thought was the Rascal,' explained the Big Cheese. 'When you moved towards him … I mean, the gun looked so real … I breathed out in horror … and that was when my stomach suddenly swelled. How was I to know that the sheer size of my belly would be enough to make my braces stretch … and stretch … and stretch … until …' The Big Cheese closed his eyes and shivered. 'They made a horrible noise when they snapped,' he said slowly. 'It was like a gun shot. Then the pain hit me. The pain of those bursting braces as they pinched my skin. It was unbearable. The only thing I can compare it to is picking your nose with a particularly jagged fingernail. Or someone else's jagged fingernail. Or even—'

'Still, at least you're alright now,' I said, grabbing the Chief of SICK under his armpits.

'Am I?' The Big Cheese refused to budge. 'I've had a nasty shock,' he insisted. 'It was quite traumatic. And what about my braces?'

'Your braces are no concern of mine,' I replied. 'Although that might change if your trousers keep on falling down.' I tried again and this time the Big Cheese let me help him to his feet. 'I know where we are,' I continued. 'Hag's Hole. And this,' I said, gesturing around the room, 'is the Rascal's Bedroom.'

With the Big Cheese strong enough to stand up by himself, I pushed past the dummy and made my way towards the door. I had already pressed down on the handle when I felt a tug on my waistcoat.

'Be prepared, young Dare,' warned the Big Cheese. 'Anything could be waiting for us outside. Friend or foe, we have to be ready to fight.' The Big Cheese hesitated. 'And for that reason, I'll let you go first,' he said, shoving me in the back. 'I mean, normally I'd be at the head of the queue, as eager as a beaver, but I am feeling a little delicate right now, especially after everything that's happened ...'

'I understand, sir.' I cut the Big Cheese off before he could embarrass himself any further. This was it. The Rascal wasn't going to catch himself and time was running away from us.

It was now or never.

I chose now and stepped outside.

31.'HAVE YOU LOST YOUR MARBLES?'

I was back where it had first begun.

Hag's Hole.

The most haunted house in the whole of Crooked Elbow.

Except it wasn't. Haunted, I mean. Not really. It was just rundown and ruined and far too big for its own good.

I looked over my shoulder and saw the Big Cheese peeking around the door. 'Is it safe?'

'As safe as houses,' I replied. 'Although that doesn't necessarily include this house which could collapse at any moment. Don't panic, though; there's nobody lurking in the shadows, ready to pounce. As for Hettie, she never comes up to the tower.'

'Hettie?' The Big Cheese stroked his moustache. 'You mean Hettie the Hag? I thought she was as dead as a doughnut.'

'That's what everybody thinks,' I said. 'But she's not. She's perfectly alive. At least she was this morning. We should probably go and check up on her, though. Just in case.'

I made my way towards the stairs. The Big Cheese followed, but at a distance. That way if anybody happened to jump out on us they would hit me first.

'So, this is Hag's Hole,' he muttered. 'You wouldn't choose to live here, would you?'

'We might not,' I said in agreement, 'but the Rascal did.'

'Yes, but that still doesn't explain why he would take us to his bedroom and leave us there,' remarked the Big Cheese. 'And what has he done with Detective Inspector Spite and Diamond Duke?'

'Those two are the least of our worries,' I shrugged. 'They're not even on our trouble timetable … our distress diary … our problem planner. But you are right; the actions of the Rascal are impossible to explain. A lot like most things in Crooked Elbow if I'm being honest.'

I hopped off the bottom step and veered towards the room without the broken floorboards. That was where I found Hettie. She was tied to the rocking chair with a gag over her mouth and a blindfold over her eyes.

I rushed over and quickly removed them both. 'Are you okay?'

It took Hettie a moment or two before she spoke. 'Am now,' she said, smiling weakly. 'Knew you would back. Was right as well, wasn't I?'

'Kind of,' I had to admit. 'It was actually the Rascal that brought us here. And I'm guessing it was the Rascal that did this to you.'

'Possibly possible,' said Hettie, as I set to work on the ties around her wrists. 'Never even saw him popping up. But he did leave me this …'

Hettie held out her hand as the ties fell away. She was holding something that I had seen far too many times that day already. Something that promised so much, but always seemed to deliver so little.

It was another paper scroll.

I took it from Hettie, unrolled it and began to read.

To the spy who seeks me,

The Day of the Rascal is nearly over. There is still time, however, for my final hurrah, my coup de grace, my perfect end to a perfect day. I had no intention of killing the Big Cheese – why would I? But I am planning on pulling off something so audacious that the sad souls of Crooked Elbow will talk about it for years to come. You'll find me at the SICK Bucket. Stop me if you can … but you can't.

Bad luck and best wishes, the Rascal.

I passed the scroll to the Big Cheese, who became increasingly alarmed with every word he read.

'This is terrible,' he roared. 'Disastrous. Probably the worst news I've ever come across whilst I've been Chief of SICK.'

'I wouldn't go that far,' I frowned.

'We need to leave.' Throwing the scroll into the air, the Big Cheese had already dashed out of the room before the words had left his mouth. 'Now!' he shouted.

'I don't think we do,' I replied.

'Why would you say that?' The Big Cheese poked his head around the door. 'Whatever the Rascal is planning it can only end badly for SICK,' he boomed. 'That is, unless we get to the SICK Bucket before it happens. We're the only ones who can end this, young Dare. We need to put a stop to the Day of the Rascal, we need to make sure it never happens again and we need to catch the Rascal once and for all.'

'I didn't know you were so *needy*, sir,' I said.

'This your granddad, Weaselly?' asked Hettie, finally deciding to join the conversation.

'Bit rude,' grumbled the Big Cheese. 'Do I look that old?'

'No, you're right,' nodded Hettie, looking the Chief of SICK up and down. 'Great granddad it is then. Can see that now. Very wrinkly up close, you are. In need of fresh air and lots of it.'

'Still rude,' remarked the Big Cheese, before switching his attention back to me. 'Have you lost your marbles?'

'Not unless there's a hole in these trousers,' I replied.

'You read the scroll,' the Big Cheese roared. 'We need to get back to the SICK Bucket—'

'We don't,' I insisted.

'We do,' growled the Big Cheese.

'We do … *not*,' I argued. Maybe now wasn't the best time to try and be funny. Before I had even finished, history seemed to repeat itself as the Big Cheese turned his back on me and hurried out of the room. This time, however, I doubted he'd come back.

'Better get after your great granddad,' remarked Hettie, gesturing towards the door. 'Don't worry about me. Be fine, I will. Just promise me one thing before you go bye-byes. Promise me you'll come back to Hag's Hole when all this is over and out.'

'Of course I will,' I said, smiling at Hettie. With that, I set off after my great granddad – also known as the Big Cheese – before he took a wrong turning and got lost amongst the cobwebs of Hag's Hole.

I spotted him halfway down the stairs. He hadn't got far, but that was hardly surprising. Not with those broken braces.

'Wait!' I called out.

'What for?' snapped the Big Cheese, as he finally reached the bottom. 'You're talking nonsense, young Dare, and I'm not listening!'

'I'm not and you should be,' I argued. 'Let me explain. I met someone—'

'Well, I hope you'll be very happy together,' muttered the Big Cheese.

'She lives in a cabin in the woods of Back O'Beyond,' I continued. 'She used to be a spy. Her name is Lady Winifred Hyde.'

The Big Cheese stopped in the hallway. 'Ding-dong,' he said bizarrely. 'Her name does ring a bell, but she was long before my time. From what I've heard, though, she was good at her job. One of the best.'

'She gave me some advice,' I continued. 'In fact, she gave me lots of advice, but one piece stuck out in particular. She told me that things aren't always what they seem. And *this* is one of those things.' I stopped to think. Something was bugging me, but I couldn't quite put my finger on it (nor any other body part come to that).

'We're wasting time,' moaned the Big Cheese. 'I shouldn't even be here as it is—'

'Stop!' I lunged at the Chief of SICK and pressed a finger to his lips. 'Stop … and then rewind.'

'I'll rewind you in a minute,' warned the Big Cheese, pushing me away. 'I'll rewind you back to a time before I made you a spy—'

'Don't say that,' I cried. 'Or anything else for that matter. Just tell me what you said before. At the beginning.'

'At the beginning?' The Big Cheese scrunched up his brow, deep in thought. 'I don't know … something like … we're wasting time,' he repeated slowly. 'And then … I shouldn't even be here—'

'That's it!' I clapped my hands together in delight. 'Why?' I asked. 'Why shouldn't you be here?'

'I should be at the River Deep monitoring everything that happens,' the Big Cheese revealed. 'Have you forgotten about Deadly De'Ath? He's being transferred to Sol's Solitary Slammer by boat tonight.'

And that was when it hit me. Hard. So hard, in fact, that I couldn't help but blurt it out. 'The Rascal isn't on his way to the SICK Bucket,' I remarked. 'He's going to the River Deep. He's going to try and free Deadly De'Ath.'

The Big Cheese started to frown. 'Are you sure?'

'No,' I had to admit. 'Not in the slightest. But that

doesn't mean I'm not right.'

'Doesn't it?' argued the Big Cheese.

'No,' I insisted. 'It's your choice, sir. The SICK Bucket or the River Deep? But remember one thing before you make your decision. We no longer have to stop the Rascal from killing you … but we do have to stop Deadly De'Ath from escaping!'

32. 'IT'S ONE OF US.'

We left Hag's Hole and set off for the River Deep by foot.

I could tell by the Big Cheese's face that he wasn't convinced. It was all scrunched up, you see. Hideously deformed. Almost as if his underpants were on too tight.

I talked all the way to take his mind off it. I told him about Mysterious Melvin's Museum of Mind-Bending Marvels … the diamond train to Twisted Kneecap … Junkin' Jack's Scrap Shack … Back O'Beyond and Lady Winifred Hyde … and, last but not least, the Wonderful World of Warehouses, right up until the moment we met. As enjoyable as they all weren't, I hadn't visited any of those peculiar places through choice. No, I had gone there because I had been instructed to. Instructed by a series of scrolls written by a person who I was still yet to meet. A person who had never been seen in twenty-seven years in fact.

The entire day had been one long, wild goose chase. Without the wild goose. But with a Rascal instead. A Rascal that had been mis-directing me every step of the way.

Had.

But not anymore.

'They'll be no coming back from this if you're wrong, young Dare,' grumbled the Big Cheese, as we hurried along the pavement. 'You'll be thrown out of SICK for good!'

'If I'm wrong, sir,' I replied, 'there won't even be a SICK!'

'Good point, well made,' the Big Cheese admitted. Without warning, he bent over and put his hands on his knees. He was struggling to breathe. 'Maybe I should ring Rumble and ask him to pick us up,' he panted. 'It's not like he'll need any transport. He can just carry us. One in the palm of each hand. Comfort guaranteed.'

'It's sounds tempting, sir, but there's not enough time,' I said. 'Besides, I've got a much better idea. It's the perfect way to travel—'

'Well, don't keep it to yourself,' cried the Big Cheese excitedly. 'I'm all ears …'

'Just two will be fine,' I insisted. 'And two feet. You'll need them to help you run … no, don't look like that, sir. Let me finish … now, I'm no expert, but it can't be that much of a trek to the River Deep. A few miles at most. If we run all the way we should easily make it there before the guards from the Crooked Clink. That way, when the Rascal makes his move and tries to free Deadly De'Ath, we can stop him. It'll be game over and goodnight. Easy-peasy, Biggy-Cheesy.' I hesitated, unsure whether or not I had overstepped the mark. 'What do you think, sir?' I asked warily.

'What do I think?' The Big Cheese stopped panting, stood up straight and puffed out his chest. 'I think, what are we waiting for?' he boomed. A moment later he was off, his bum wiggling in time with his footsteps as he shuffled slowly along the pavement. 'We're SICK,' he shouted back at me. 'Simply the best. No, we're better than that. We can do this. We can do anything. And that, young Dare, is a fact.'

We couldn't. And it wasn't.

Don't get me wrong. We did get to the River Deep – eventually – but we didn't run. Not after the first few steps anyway. If I'm being honest, we barely walked. Well, one of us didn't.

And that one of us wasn't me.

Despite his rallying cry, the Big Cheese limped most of the way there like a three-week-old lettuce leaf in a heatwave. That was bad enough, but worse was to come when I offered to give him a piggy back. To my horror, the Chief of SICK was even heavier than he looked … and, believe me when I say, that should not have been possible!

In the end, it took us fifty-seven long minutes to reach our destination. The time was fast approaching eight, but only a fool would rush in now (no, don't say that. You know it's not true). With that in mind, I slowed my step and approached the River Deep at a much gentler pace, something that suited the Big Cheese just fine. By the time we had got there, in fact, he had even found the breath to string a few words together.

'This is your mission, young Dare,' he whispered, 'so you make the rules. What now?'

'Now we wait.' I stopped talking and took a look around. The road that had brought us here had come to an abrupt halt, leaving nothing but a loose trail that led down to the river. Aside from that, there wasn't a single building in sight and precious little lighting to guide us on our way. 'I'm guessing the Rascal hasn't arrived yet,' I said, 'but he'll have to get here soon if he's going to free Deadly De'Ath—'

The Big Cheese made a noise like a disgruntled toad. 'And if he doesn't …?'

I chose to ignore that as I made my way towards the riverbank. The closer we got to the water, the darker our surroundings seemed to get, so much so that, after only a few steps, I could no longer see what was beneath my feet. Not until it was too late at least.

Too late being the moment I tripped over and fell flat on my face.

'That sounded painful,' snorted the Big Cheese, helping me up off the ground.

'It was.' I stepped back and ran my hand across the grass, interested to know what had sent me tumbling. What I found was a length of rope. One end had been hammered into the riverbank with a metal peg. I followed it all the way to the edge of the river and saw that it was attached to something floating in the water.

A rowing boat.

'Don't tell me that Deadly De'Ath is being transported in that?' I groaned.

'Then I won't,' replied the Big Cheese. 'But, just in case you're wondering, he is. What's wrong with it?'

'It's a bit … it's a bit …' I struggled to think of a way to finish that particular sentence, so decided not to. *A bit* was exactly what the boat was. Just *a bit*. Nothing more, nothing less.

'Deadly De'Ath doesn't deserve to travel in style,' remarked the Big Cheese. 'He's a prisoner and this is part of his punishment. Besides, if he tries to escape he'll drown in the river, and if he doesn't then in six hours and forty-seven minutes time he'll find himself at Sol's Solitary Slammer.'

'What's it like?' I asked.

'Lonely,' revealed the Big Cheese. 'There's nobody else there except for Sol … and he doesn't tend to say much. Nothing nice, anyway. No small talk. Just swear words. His favourite is … what's that?'

I followed the Big Cheese's finger as he pointed over my shoulder. There was a light in the distance, jumping about in a jerky fashion. A torch perhaps. It seemed to stop suddenly when the road ended before it turned towards the riverbank.

'That might be the Rascal,' I said nervously. 'We should hide before we scare him off.'

'Easier said than done,' muttered the Big Cheese. Unfortunately, he was right. I searched high and low (mostly low if I'm being honest, strictly ground level), but there was no sign of anything even half-resembling a hiding place anywhere near us.

Except …

Reaching down, I picked up the rope from beneath my feet and gave it a good yank. At the same time, the boat moved. I continued to pull until it glided all the way back to dry land. My plan had worked. I had found us a hiding place.

'Enjoying yourself?' asked the Big Cheese, confused.

'Not particularly.' I gestured towards the boat as it came to a halt at the bank. 'Why don't you hop in and try it out for size?' I suggested.

'It doesn't look very comfy,' moaned the Big Cheese. He straightened his cravat, took a breath and then scrambled onboard. I quickly joined him before pushing against the bank with my trailing leg. The force was enough to send us sliding back into the water. We drifted for a while until the rope began to tighten. We were no more than five metres away from the bank when I realised the boat had floated back to the exact same point where I had first spotted it.

By now, the torch light had almost reached the water's edge. As expected, there was a shadowy figure right behind it. If I looked hard enough I could just about make out dark clothing … gloves … and a thick head of spiky hair.

I knew who it was.

'Get down, young Dare,' urged the Big Cheese. 'The Rascal will see you.'

'But that's not the Rascal,' I insisted. 'It's one of us.'

'One of us?' The Big Cheese squinted into the darkness. 'Well, it's definitely not me … and I don't think it's you … so that just leaves … no, I'm stumped. You'll have to spell it out for me, I'm afraid.'

'It's Violet Crow,' I said, waving at the shadowy figure. 'Agent Sixteen. She's one of your agents.'

'She?' The Big Cheese stopped squinting and shrugged his shoulders instead. 'She's one of my agents?'

'That what I said, sir,' I nodded. 'It is quite flattering I suppose, but you don't have to repeat everything I say.'

'I'm only repeating it because it's complete and utter claptrap,' argued the Big Cheese. 'Yes, Violet Crow is a master of disguise, but that's not Violet Crow. That's a whole different person altogether.'

I screwed up my face. 'No … you're wrong … look again … she's been helping me all day.'

'She might have been,' admitted the Big Cheese, 'but Violet Crow certainly hasn't. Not only is Violet Crow a man, but he's also been missing for most of the day. He went off radar shortly before he was supposed to meet you at Hag's Hole. He was disguised as a jogger.'

The memory of that morning hit me so hard I almost fell off the boat. 'A jogger?' I mumbled.

'You've got a lot of explaining to do, young Dare … starting with her.' The Big Cheese pointed towards the woman on the riverbank, the woman who up until two seconds ago I had believed was Violet Crow. 'Who … is … she?' he asked slowly.

33. 'YOU'RE NOT A VERY GOOD SHOT, ARE YOU?'

Good question.

For once I didn't know what to say. The woman who had been working alongside me all day wasn't Violet Crow. She wasn't Agent Sixteen. She wasn't even SICK. And yet she had been there every step of the way. Helping and assisting me. Coming to my rescue.

Hadn't she?

I watched in disbelief as Crow – or whoever she really was – came to a halt at the edge of the riverbank and peered out at the rowing boat that the Big Cheese and I were trying – and failing – to hide in.

'This is an unexpected surprise,' she said, smiling to herself. That was a worry for a start. Crow never smiled. 'Now you I recognise, Weasel,' she continued, 'but who's that beside you? He looks too old to be your granddad …'

'Why do people keep on saying that?' moaned the Big Cheese. 'It's just the job I do. It's very stressful. And I don't get much sleep. Or exercise. And my diet's atrocious. All that pizza …' The Big Cheese stopped suddenly so he could whisper in my ear. 'Don't tell her who I am, young Dare.'

'I won't, sir,' I whispered back. Then I turned to Crow. 'I'm not telling you who he is,' I shouted. 'He could be anyone. Anyone in the whole of Crooked Elbow. Anyone but the Chief of SICK. Definitely not him. No way.'

The Big Cheese rolled his eyes in despair. 'Well done, young Dare,' he sighed. 'That wasn't really, really obvious, was it?'

The counterfeit Crow put a hand to her mouth. 'Oh, how exciting,' she said, mocking us. 'I should feel honoured. I wasn't expecting to find the Big Cheese and his stupidest spy here waiting for me. I suppose it's only fair that I tell you who I am before we get down to business. My name is Layla Krool—'

'No, it's not,' I blurted out. 'And it's not Violet Crow either. I know exactly who you are. You're the Rascal. And you have been all along.'

'Me? The Rascal?' Layla Krool began to laugh. 'I can see why a pea-brain like you might think that, but there's a good reason why it's not true. Now, I don't want this to come as too much of a shock, Weasel, but the Rascal doesn't actually exist.'

'Well, that's where you're wrong,' argued the Big Cheese. 'If the Rascal didn't exist then neither would the Day of the Rascal. But that does exist. Because it's today. End of conversation.'

'Wow! That was a convincing argument,' smirked Krool. 'Consider me won over … not! Okay, you two dimwits, let's get one thing straight. The Day of the Rascal is made up. It's make believe. Fabricated, fictional and completely fake. No one really knows when it is or bothers to celebrate it. It's like Grandparent's Day. Or International Monkey Cuddling Day.'

'How dare you!' boomed the Big Cheese. 'International Monkey Cuddling Day is my favourite day of the year.'

'Oh, please,' groaned Krool. 'The Day of the Rascal is not a real day … and the Rascal is not a real person. He or she is just a myth. A legend that has grown over time until the foolish people in Crooked Elbow eventually believed it. All those jokes and pranks and accidents that have happened over the years are just lots and lots of different rogues and wrong 'uns making mischief. Nothing more than that.'

'What about the paper scrolls?' I asked, confused. 'The Rascal kept on leaving them for me—'

'No, *I* kept on leaving them for you,' revealed Krool. 'Nobody else. Pretty obvious when you think about it. Didn't you find it odd that I was always there whenever the scrolls appeared? Sometimes I barely had time to put them down before you showed up. Once or twice I even handed them to you.'

'Well, when you put it like that …' I had to admit. 'But I trusted you. You were Agent Sixteen. We were on the same team. Or so I thought.'

'Sorry to disappoint you, Weasel,' shrugged Krool, 'but that's not all. Everything else that has happened today has been down to me as well. The dummy in Hag's Hole. The unconscious security guard and missing skateboard in

Mysterious Melvin's Museum of Mind-Bending Marvels. Junkin' Jack's runaway caravan. The poisonous smoke in the M.T. warehouse. I've been very busy, but it's all been worth it.'

'Has it?' I asked, struggling to make sense of what was happening. 'Because I can't see the point—'

'The point?' Krool started to laugh. A high-pitched cackle, it was even worse than when she smiled. 'The point was to distract you,' she revealed. 'Everything today has been done to baffle and bewilder you. To steer you off course and then keep you heading in the wrong direction. I even threw in Detective Inspector Spite and the Majestic Mob to confuse things further. You've had a very strange day, Weasel … and it was all because of me! As for you …' Krool gestured rudely towards the Big Cheese. 'You've been so worried about being killed that you took your eye off the ball.'

'What ball?' asked the Big Cheese.

'Exactly,' said Krool. 'I never wanted to kill you. Why would I? You're not important. Deadly De'Ath, however, is. He means everything to me.' Krool shivered with excitement. 'I'm his number two,' she said proudly.

'I tend to leave my number twos in the toilet,' I muttered.

'I'm his second in command,' continued Krool, ignoring me. 'That's why I need him back. We all need him back. Crooked Elbow's criminal community isn't the same without him. He's the glue that binds us all together.'

'He always was a particularly sticky character,' frowned the Big Cheese.

'He's the best,' gushed Krool. 'The best at being the worst. We couldn't just let him rot in Sol's Solitary Slammer for the rest of his life. What a waste that would be! Deadly De'Ath is the ball you took your eye off,' revealed Krool, wagging a finger at the Big Cheese. 'How … careless. How … unprofessional. How very … very … stupid.' Krool stopped and looked over her shoulder as a set of headlights appeared in the road behind her. 'Oh, here they are now,' she said, beaming with delight. 'Right on time. I should probably go and introduce myself. Hello, I'm Violet Crow. Agent Sixteen. I'll take Deadly De'Ath from here on in, thank you very much.'

Now it was my turn to laugh. 'They won't just hand him over to you.'

'Won't they?' argued Krool. 'Don't forget; you believed me. So why won't they?'

I hated to admit it, but she had a point. 'It won't work,' I said, trying to convince myself as much as anyone. 'It might be dark and we are quite faraway, but the guards from the Crooked Clink will still see us and the boat and then they'll know there's something wrong.'

'Yes, I did wonder about that …' Quick as a flash, Krool bent down and untied the rope that I had tripped over. With nothing holding it in place, the boat began to drift off into the water. 'So long,' she called out. 'Today's been a lot of fun, but nothing lasts forever. Oh, just one thing before I go …'

Reaching into her pocket, Krool removed a small handgun.

'Whoa!' I said, holding up my hands. 'There's no need for—'

Krool fired off a shot before I could finish my sentence. I tensed up, fearing the worst, but felt nothing that would make my fears come true. Even the Big Cheese seemed to be okay. Yes, he was on his knees, but he didn't look to be in any pain. 'Have you been hit, sir?' I asked.

'Not as far as I'm aware,' said the Big Cheese, patting himself all over. 'Although I wouldn't imagine it would hurt as much as those blooming braces even if I had.'

I turned back to Krool and smiled. 'You're not a very good shot, are you?'

'Oh, I'm a very good shot,' replied Krool. With that, she made her way back up the riverbank towards the road.

'Young Dare, I don't know how to tell you this, but we've got a problem,' remarked the Big Cheese.

'We've got lots of problems,' I grumbled.

'Not like this one,' the Big Cheese insisted. 'This is a particularly wet worry.'

I was about to ask what he meant when I felt water sploshing between my toes. I looked down and saw something in the boat that hadn't been there before Krool had fired.

It was a hole.

Layla Krool was right; she *was* a good shot. Firing at me or the Big Cheese wasn't her intention at all. No, she had been aiming for the boat. She was trying to sink it. And, no doubt, sink us at the same time.

But that wasn't about to happen.

'Don't panic, sir,' I said calmly. 'All we have to do is swim back to dry land and—'

'That's the problem,' groaned the Big Cheese, wrapping his arms around his body to stop himself from trembling. 'I can't swim!'

34.'SPY OVERBOARD!'

I watched as the headlights ground to a halt in the distance.

I guessed it was an armoured van. White in colour and at least twice the size of a car, it wasn't the kind of thing that Layla Krool could easily break into. Not that she needed to, of course. As far as she was concerned, all she had to do was knock on the window and tell the guards who she was (or, rather, who she was pretending to be) and then they would hand over Deadly De'Ath. Whether that was true or not, I had no idea, but I did know one thing. Just bumbling around on the boat, hoping for the best, wasn't a risk worth taking. Somehow, I had to stop her.

First, however, I had to deal with the Big Cheese. And it wasn't quite as simple as pulling a pair of armbands out of my pocket and pushing him into the River Deep before the boat sank.

'You can't swim?' I repeated, just to be sure.

The Big Cheese shook his moustache. 'Afraid not, young Dare,' he admitted. 'If I'm being honest, I've spent most of my life avoiding water. Lakes … streams … puddles … bird baths … you name it, I've steered well clear of it. Even watering cans have been known to give me the shivers. I mean, being able to swim was never one of the requirements when I became the Chief of SICK—'

'Until now,' I sighed. I watched Layla Krool as she made her way across the road towards the armoured van. I was supposed to be doing something to stop her, but I was still in watching mode. Watching *and* thinking. There had to be a way of getting the Big Cheese safely out of the water. If only I had something long and thin that I could use to pull the rowing boat back to the riverbank …

'Have you still got that walking stick your father made for me?' asked the Big Cheese, out of the blue. 'It might be long enough to pull us back to the riverbank.'

Talk about a coincidence …

I winked at the Big Cheese before reaching inside my trousers. I knew the walking stick extended a long way, but how long was that? I guessed there was only one way to find out …

Leaning over the side of the boat, I held the stick at arm's length and flicked my wrist with as much force as I could muster. I had spotted a particularly stubborn root poking out of the bank that was perfect for what I had in mind. If I could hook the handle around it, I'd be able to pull us through the water. Back to dry land. Just in time to stop Layla Krool.

Convinced it would work, I followed the flight of the walking stick as it soared through the air before its sudden descent. To my dismay, the handle fell short and didn't even make it to the riverbank.

'Bad luck, young Dare,' roared the Big Cheese. 'Why don't you try leaning over a little more?'

'I'll pretend I didn't hear that,' I muttered. The walking stick was dripping wet as I dragged it out of the water. 'You could always have a go yourself if you think you could do better.'

'Not likely!' the Big Cheese boomed. 'I might fall in!'

'So might I,' I snapped back at him.

'Exactly, young Dare,' nodded the Big Cheese. 'Rather you than me. Obviously.'

'Obviously,' I groaned. I placed a foot on the side of the rowing boat and it began to wobble. As did my nerves. I was all set to try again with the walking stick when I heard a shrill laugh in the distance. Looking over, I saw Layla Krool resting against the armoured van, chatting to the guard in the driver's seat. They seemed to be getting on.

With no time to waste, I threw out my arm and hoped with all my heart that the stick would be long enough.

It wasn't.

Not for the first time, it fell short. On this occasion, however, it did reach the riverbank. I had missed the root, but I was getting closer.

The sound of a slamming door in the distance drew my attention. The driver had climbed out of their seat, before moving towards the back of the van. I couldn't be certain (a combination of poor light, tired eyes and a wobbly boat saw to that) but I guessed it was a man … and he was doing exactly what Krool wanted.

'Grab my legs,' I ordered.

'What with?' asked the Big Cheese.

'Your hands, of course,' I cried.

'Oh, that won't be possible,' replied the Big Cheese awkwardly. 'My hands are currently occupied. They're … um … busy. Busy covering my eyes.'

I screwed up my face. Then I screwed it up some more when I saw that the driver and Krool had been re-united at the front of the van. Now, however, there was somebody else.

Somebody covered head to toe in a white blanket with chains wrapped around their body.

It was the prisoner.

The prisoner who had to be Deadly De'Ath.

One way or another, I had to get off the boat. And fast.

Placing both feet on the side, I swung the stick towards the bank before my balance deserted me for good. The stick brushed against the root and then fell away. I was so close it was starting to irritate me. I had to try again. One more go.

With nothing to lose, I leant over more than I dared … and then a little bit more after that. Yes, I was desperate, but that didn't make it the right thing to do. I realised that a moment later when, somewhat predictably, the boat began to tip, my feet couldn't help but slip and the rest of my body did some kind of gold-medal-winning flip. That was where the rhyming all but ended. No, now I was just falling.

Straight into the River Deep.

'Spy overboard!' bellowed the Big Cheese.

I made a huge splash as first my head, and then my shoulders, disappeared under the surface. I quickly rolled over and let my feet pad around for a while, but I couldn't quite find the bottom. Surprise surprise, the River Deep had lived up to its name. Not to worry. I could easily have panicked, but chose instead to use the strength in my arms to drive myself up and out of the water.

It seemed to take forever, but my head eventually rose above the surface.

'Bravo, young Dare?' cheered the Big Cheese. 'Is it cold in there?'

I refused to answer (largely because I didn't want to admit that it was). More than you could ever imagine, in fact. So cold that my eyelashes had frozen solid and my tongue felt like an ice lolly. Still, now I had taken the plunge there was no point getting out. Not yet, anyway. Not until I had reached the riverbank.

I got there twelve strokes later. Throwing the walking stick to one side, I dug my fingers into the mud and tried desperately to haul myself out of the water. The over-sized clothes were like a dead weight around me, pulling my body under the surface, but eventually I did it. I was back on dry land. But there was no time to waste.

With my face buried in the riverbank, I began to half-crawl, half-slither towards the road. I moved slowly at first (and second and third), but at least I was moving. I stopped when the shouting started. I knew without looking that it was the Big Cheese. He sounded terrified, but then so would I if my only hope of escaping from a sinking boat had just swum off and left me to it.

'Watch out, young Dare … watch out … watch out …'

It took longer than it should have for my brain to make sense of what he was saying. At least six seconds. Six seconds for me to realise that I was wrong. Wrong to think that the Big Cheese was begging for me to save him.

No, what he was actually doing was warning me.

Warning me about what was about to happen.

And I had ignored him.

35.'UNTIL WE MEET AGAIN.'

Fearing the worst, I lifted my face out of the riverbank so I could see what all the fuss was about.

The armoured van may have gone, but now there were two pairs of feet only inches away from my eyeballs.

One pair were hidden inside black boots. They belonged to Layla Krool. The other pair, however, were completely bare and splattered with mud. I glanced up a little more and saw they were attached to the prisoner from the armoured van. The prisoner who was draped in a thick blanket and wrapped up in chains.

The prisoner who I couldn't let escape under any circumstances.

I tried to push myself up, but Krool stood on my back and my arms gave way.

'This is the spy I told you about, Your Deadliness,' she said scornfully. 'His name is Pink Weasel. He works for SICK. He's been very persistent today. Like a dog with a bone. Not a particularly clever dog, of course, but he's never given up. Not once. It's a quality I know you admire.'

The prisoner in the chains – the man I now knew to be

criminal genius Deadly De'Ath – didn't reply. Instead, he began to shuffle his feet from side-to-side whilst swivelling his hips like a hula hooper minus the hula hoop.

'I think he might need the toilet,' I remarked.

'I'd lay off the jokes if I was you, Weasel,' scowled Krool. 'You should count your blessings that Deadly De'Ath is in a good mood. That's why he's dancing. He'll probably start singing as well if we stay here long enough. You seem to be forgetting that he's a free man now. He can do what he likes, whenever he wants, starting with seeing his daughter. Fatale De'Ath is the love of his life. Talking of which …' Krool rested a glove on the prisoner's shoulder. 'There's something else, Your Deadliness,' she began. 'Fatale met the spy called Weasel whilst you were away. They ran around Elbow's End together, making mischief. She found him … amusing.'

'She liked laughing at me if that's what you mean,' I muttered under my breath. 'But I'll be the only one who's laughing when your little escape plan goes horribly wrong and the two of you end up behind bars in the Crooked Clink.'

'Is that so?' snorted Krool. 'And who's going to make that happen, Weasel? You? I don't think so somehow! You're nothing but a shrivelled up schoolboy in a wet waistcoat. And as for the Big Cheese, he's so old and slow he couldn't even catch a cold. He's a dinosaur from SICK's past. Look at him. He's so useless he can't even get off that boat.'

'Yes, I can,' insisted the Big Cheese, climbing gingerly to his feet. The boat began to sink a little more so he sat back down again. 'I just don't want to,' he mumbled. 'I like it on here. I'm … erm … chilling. As for you two rotters,' he said, pointing feebly at De'Ath and Krool, 'this is where your evening ends. You're not going anywhere. Isn't that right, young Dare?'

'Bit late for that now, sir,' I groaned. Digging my hands into the mud, I tried again to push myself up, but Krool was quick to swipe my arms away with her boot.

'Be seeing you, Weasel,' she smirked. 'Until we meet again …'

I reached out and tried to grab Krool's ankles as she turned to leave, but my fingers fell away as she kicked out with her boot. When I looked again she was already clambering up the riverbank with the blanketed Deadly De'Ath at her side. I knew then that there was nothing I could do. In a blink of an eye they would disappear into the darkness.

I blinked.

And they were gone.

'Young Dare!' called out the Big Cheese. 'Have you forgotten there's a hole in this boat?'

Unfortunately, I had. Not that I'd ever admit it. Instead, I rolled onto my back for a better view of the River Deep. Half of the boat was now completely under the surface of the water whilst the Big Cheese perched awkwardly at the other end.

The boat was sinking fast … and, if I wasn't careful, the Chief of SICK would go down with it.

'Get ready, sir!' I crawled across the riverbank and grabbed the walking stick that Krool had kicked away. With a flick of my wrist, it extended across the river towards the rowing boat. Shaking like a human jelly, the Big Cheese managed to catch it with both hands and then refused to let go. I began to pull; unsure what would happen next. Either the Big Cheese would just fall into the water, or the boat would begin to drift back towards me.

To my relief, it was the latter of the two.

'Splendid work, young Dare,' boomed the Big Cheese, as the boat finally shuddered to a halt not far from where I had just been laid on the riverbank. 'You're safe … and that's good. But I'm safe, too … and that's what really matters!'

'What about Deadly De'Ath?' I was so exhausted I could barely speak. A long day may have been coming to an end, but it wasn't coming to an end the way I wanted. 'I let him escape.'

'Did you?' the Big Cheese shrugged. At the same time, he lifted a leaking leg and climbed clumsily out of the boat. 'I didn't realise,' he admitted. 'I don't know if you were aware but I had more watery worries weighing me down. No, losing Deadly De'Ath is hardly ideal, young Dare, but it's nothing to get your pants in a pickle about. We've caught him once; we can catch him again. And then if he escapes, we'll catch him again. And then if he escapes after that, we can always—'

'Yes, I get it, sir,' I said, shivering with every word. My clothes were dripping wet and there was no way they would ever dry in the cold Crooked Elbow air.

'We need to get you home,' insisted the Big Cheese. 'I'll call Rumble. He can come and pick us up. And if he hasn't got the car he can always bring a wheelbarrow. He's good, like that. Very reliable. What's wrong with your face now, young Dare? It's even worse than usual. Unnecessarily ugly, in fact.'

'It's only ugly because we failed, sir,' I said sadly.

'I'm not sure we did,' argued the Big Cheese. Throwing an arm over my shoulder, he led me up the riverbank, away from the River Deep. 'Let me put it another way. We may have lost our shopping list, but that doesn't mean we can't buy any more groceries. Okay, so Deadly De'Ath has temporarily escaped, but at least we won't have to worry about the Day of the Rascal ever again. Oh, and I'm still alive. That's the best news of all.' The Big Cheese took a breath. 'I'm actually feeling really rather cheerful about things,' he boomed. 'As long as there are spies like me around, the fine folk of Crooked Elbow can rest easy in their beds at night.'

'Don't forget about me, sir,' I said, my loafers squelching with every step as I made my way back onto the road.

'Yes, you too, young Dare,' agreed the Big Cheese, patting me gently on the head. 'You can rest easy in your bed as well.'

36.'WE'RE NOT AS DAFT AS WE LOOK.'

The next morning I was interrupted mid-slumber by the hideous howl of two cats ripping the hairballs out of each other.

I couldn't tell if it was the same two cats as the day before (or even if it was the same hairballs), but the outcome was unfortunately the same. I was awake.

It was Sunday. Four forty-nine in the morning to be precise. Early, yes, but still a lie-in compared to twenty-four hours ago when I had risen at four forty-one. Sitting up in bed, I vigorously rubbed my nostrils until I remembered it was my eyes that I was supposed to be rubbing and my nose just needed a good pick. Once I had done both to an adequate standard, I climbed feet-first into my dressing gown and hung my slippers from my ears. Maybe I was still half-asleep, but the day hadn't got off to the best of starts. A lot like yesterday, in fact.

There was one thing, however, that would spark my senses, tickle my taste buds and set me up for what was to come. And, thankfully, it didn't involve me licking the crusty bits out the corners of my own eye sockets.

No, it was breakfast.

And I knew just where to find it.

The cats had stopped arguing, shaken paws and gone their separate ways by the time I had squeezed past the lawnmower and stepped out of my shedroom (that's a shed-cum-bedroom for those of you with short-term memory loss). It was another revoltingly cold morning, but I wasn't planning on hanging around outside long enough to feel the chill penetrate my pyjamas. Instead, I made my way towards the house, my mind skipping back to the events of yesterday as I trudged wearily through the grass. On that occasion, I had made three mistakes. Three mistakes that could easily have led me into a potentially fatal trap.

Today, however, I wasn't so careless.

Today I noticed that the back door was unlocked.

And that the kitchen light was on.

And that the bulging, barrel-shaped belly that was Brown Cow (also known as Agent Ten) was sat at the table.

Like the day before, he was scooping super-sized spoonfuls of my favourite cereal into the equally super-sized hole at the front of his face. Three mouthfuls later I decided to confront him before he finished the entire packet in one short sitting.

'Who said you could eat my multi-grain, choco-frosted, crunchy-crispy, sweet and sour, loopy hoops. With added prunes. And a hint of garlic?' I asked angrily.

Brown Cow looked up from his bowl and grunted. 'What was that?'

'Who said you could eat my multi-grain, choco-frosted … oh, forget it,' I sighed. 'What are you doing here?'

'That's strictly need to know,' replied a grinning Brown Cow. Without another word, he continued to work his way through breakfast. I couldn't be sure, but he seemed to be laughing under his breath. Laughing at me.

'Strictly need to know,' repeated another voice in the kitchen. I turned to see the stick-thin, hard of hearing Grey Hound lurking behind the door. Unlike Brown Cow, he wasn't grinning. But that didn't mean he wasn't just as irritating.

'I'm guessing the Big Cheese sent you both,' I said, sitting down at the table.

'Do you know what that is?' Brown Cow pretended to pause for thought. 'Strictly need to know,' he sniggered.

'And now you're going to collect and deliver me,' I continued. 'Like a human parcel … but without the wrapping paper and sticky tape.'

'Let me see … yes, that's strictly need to know as well,' said a still sniggering Brown Cow.

I screwed up my face in frustration. I didn't have to put up with this kind of nonsense.

So I decided not to.

'You do remember what happened yesterday, don't you?' I asked.

Brown Cow stopped eating and put his spoon down on the table. 'Yes, I remember,' he nodded. 'You said that when the clock struck five, you would make your move. It was going to be swift and brutal and we would both get hurt.

Badly hurt. Like *crying for our mummy* hurt. Big tears and lots of snot. Boo-hoo.'

Brown Cow couldn't hold it in anymore and burst out laughing. A moment or six later Grey Hound followed his lead. They seemed to find me funny. Their mistake.

'We're not as daft as we look,' Brown Cow remarked. 'You can't fool us with the same trick twice. There is no clock on the wall.'

'Isn't there?' I replied. 'You two need to pay more attention. Twenty-four hours is a long time in the life of a spy. Especially when my father has been busy with his hammer and nails.'

Sensing something was wrong, Brown Cow and Grey Hound both turned to look at the kitchen wall at exactly the same time, but they had left it too late.

The newly-installed clock struck five and they jumped in shock. Suddenly they were caught off guard. They weren't ready.

Unlike me.

Leaping up onto the kitchen table, I grabbed Brown Cow's bowl and balanced it in the palm of my hand.

I was about to make my move.

Advantage, Hugo Dare.

THE END

HUGO DARE WILL RETURN

IN…

THE HUNT FOR HUGO DARE

OTHER BOOKS IN THE SERIES

THE GREATEST SPY WHO NEVER WAS (HUGO DARE BOOK 1)

Meet Hugo Dare. Schoolboy turned super spy. Both stupidly dangerous and dangerously stupid.

A robbery at the Bottle Bank. Diamond smuggling at the Pearly Gates Cemetery. The theft of priceless artefact, Coocamba's Idol. Hugo is there on each and every occasion. but then so, too, is someone else.

Wrinkles, the town of Crooked Elbow's oldest criminal mastermind.

In a battle of good versus evil, young versus old, ugly versus even uglier, there can only be one winner … and it better be Hugo otherwise we're all in trouble!

To buy in the US -
https://www.amazon.com/dp/B082Z56VCR/
To buy in the UK -
https://www.amazon.co.uk/dp/B082Z56VCR/

THE WEASEL HAS LANDED (HUGO DARE BOOK 2)

Schoolboy turned super spy Hugo Dare is back … and this time he's going where others fear to tread!

No, not barefoot through a puddle of cat sick. This is much, much worse than that.

Maya, the Mayor of Crooked Elbow's daughter, is being held captive in one of the most dangerous places known to mankind.

Elbow's End.

Populated by rogues and wrong 'uns of the lowest order, only one person can find Maya and get her out of there in one piece. Unfortunately, that person is busy flossing their nostrils so it's left to someone else.

And that someone else is Hugo!

ACKNOWLEDGEMENTS

Thanks to the wonderful Sian Phillips for her eagle-eyed editing skills and glowing praise.

Thanks to the wonderful Stuart Bache and all the team at Books Covered for the front cover.

Thanks to everyone at the wonderful Polgarus Studio for their first-rate formatting.

Note to self – try and look for another word other than wonderful. Do not forget. Because that would be really embarrassing. I'm embarrassed enough already just thinking about it.

AUTHOR FACTFILE

NAME: David Codd. But you can call me David Codd. Because that's my name. Obviously.

DATE OF BIRTH: Sometime in the past. It's all a little hazy. I'm not entirely convinced I was even there if I'm being honest.

BIRTHPLACE: In a hospital. In Lincoln. In Lincolnshire. In England.

ADDRESS: No, thank you. I don't like the feel of the wind against my bare legs.

HEIGHT: Taller than a squirrel but much shorter than a lamppost. Just somewhere in between.

WEIGHT: What for?

OCCUPATION: Writing this. It doesn't just happen by magic. Or maybe it does.

LIKES: Norwich City football club, running, desert boots, parsnips.

DISLIKES: Norwich City football club, running, rain, Brussels sprouts.

REASON FOR WRITING: I wanted to give my fingers some exercise. They were getting lazy, just hanging there.

ANYTHING ELSE: Thank you for reading this book. If you've got this far then you deserve a medal. Just don't ask me for one. Because I haven't got any. But I am very grateful. And do feel free to leave a review on Amazon if leaving reviews on Amazon is your kind of thing. It's not easy for a new author so please be kind.

Until the next time …